4/17

Praise for the delightful mysteries of
Kate Kingsbury . . .

10-2-17 &B
11-12-2019 &B

"Sitting Marsh and its array of small-town citizens are realistically and humorously depicted." —*The Mystery Reader*

"Likable characters, period details, and a puzzle that kept me guessing until the end. . . . Very enjoyable."
—*Mystery News*

"Clever and cunning. . . . Delightfully unique and entertaining. A most delicious tea-time mystery with just the right atmosphere and a charming cast of characters."
—*The Literary Times*

"Always most enjoyable." —*I Love a Mystery*

"Well-drawn characters." —*Publishers Weekly*

"Full of humor, suspense, adventure, and touches of romance . . . delightful." —*Rendezvous*

"Delightful and charming." —*Painted Rock Reviews*

"Trust me, you will not be disappointed . . . Ms. Kingsbury has created a memorable series with delightful characters that can be enjoyed over and over again." —*Myshelf.com*

"Sublime. . . . Fascinating mid-twentieth-century mystery."
—*BookBrowser*

**Visit Kate Kingsbury's website at
www.doreenrobertshight.com**

W9-ASI-790

Manor House Mysteries by Kate Kingsbury

A BICYCLE BUILT FOR MURDER
DEATH IS IN THE AIR
FOR WHOM DEATH TOLLS
DIG DEEP FOR MURDER

DIG DEEP
FOR MURDER

KATE KINGSBURY

BERKLEY PRIME CRIME, NEW YORK

DIG DEEP FOR MURDER

A Berkley Prime Crime Book / published by arrangement with the author

PRINTING HISTORY
Berkley Prime Crime mass-market edition / December 2002

Copyright © 2002 by Doreen Roberts Hight.
Cover art by Dan Craig.
Cover design by Judy Murello.

Visit our website at
www.penguinputnam.com

ISBN: 0-425-18886-8

Berkley Prime Crime Books are published
by The Berkley Publishing Group,
a division of Penguin Putnam Inc.,
375 Hudson Street, New York, New York 10014.
The name BERKLEY PRIME CRIME
and the BERKLEY PRIME CRIME design
are trademarks belonging to Penguin Putnam Inc.

PRINTED IN THE UNITED STATES OF AMERICA

10 9 8 7 6 5 4 3 2 1

CHAPTER

1

"I have to find someone to take over poor John Rickett's plot," Lady Elizabeth Hartleigh Compton murmured. "I hate to see it go to weed after he took such excellent care of it. It's essential that we keep the Victory Gardens productive."

Seated at her desk in her office, she shuffled through the stack of papers in front of her. Lately it seemed that the paperwork necessary to run the Manor House and its estate was rapidly multiplying out of control.

She'd been more or less talking to herself, and didn't expect an answer. She was therefore quite surprised when Polly spoke up.

"Ooh, can me mum have it? She's been talking about growing vegetables for ages, but our garden ain't—isn't—big enough. Full of rosebushes and dahlias, it is. Me dad would have a fit if she dug that lot up to grow spuds."

1

Polly slammed the drawer of the file cabinet closed, rocking it on its feet.

The cabinet was actually an antique chest of drawers that had once graced the vast bedroom of Elizabeth's late parents, Lord and Lady Wellsborough. It wasn't accustomed to having its drawers slammed. Elizabeth had to wonder how long it could withstand her diligent assistant's treatment.

Polly sat down at the small table Elizabeth had provided for her. "I remember when the air raid wardens told us we should put a bomb shelter in the garden. Me mum told 'em it would be over her dead body. She got really, really cross when they said as how she might very well be dead without one. When she told me dad what they said—"

Well aware that if she didn't put a stop to Polly's chatter, she wouldn't get any more work out of her, Elizabeth said firmly, "Your mother is welcome to the plot as long as she utilizes it. I trust she plans to grow more than spuds—er—potatoes?"

"I s'pose so. She's always going on about how hard it is to get lettuce and tomatoes since the rationing. And she likes carrots, and peas, and cauliflower, and brussels sprouts, and—"

"Well, that's settled, then." Elizabeth scribbled the name *Edna Barnett* in the space at the top of the page. "Tell your mother that if she needs advice on growing things, Desmond will be happy to oblige."

Polly wrinkled her nose. "Not much of a gardener, that Desmond. I saw him pruning the rosebushes the other day. Just chopping at 'em, he was. Me dad would make a better gardener than Des." She propped her chin on her hand and gazed out the window. "Wish he could be your gardener instead of being in the Army. I don't half miss him."

"I'm sure you do. Desmond does his best, however. With most of the men in the village off to war, we have to make do with who and what we can get. Now, how are you getting along with those rent notices?"

Polly looked down at the register. "Still got some more to do. I see Fred Bickham's late with his rent."

"Really?" Elizabeth frowned. "How peculiar. Fred has paid his rent on time ever since he moved into that cottage. It's not like him to be late. Something must be wrong. I'll have to run down and have a chat with him."

"I could do it on me way home!" Polly looked excited at the prospect. "I'll get the money out of the old bugger, you see if I don't."

"Thank you, Polly, but I can take care of it. If Fred has a problem, I should be the one to discuss it with him."

- "Yes, m'm."

"Actually, I really need you to ring the Labour Exchange in London to see if they have any more applicants for the job of housemaid. So far no one I've interviewed seems particularly keen to take the job. I had no idea it would take all this time to find someone."

"If you ask me, it's Violet what frightens them off. Girls nowadays don't like being bossed around and spoken to like they're dirt. There's so many jobs out there for women now, they don't have to put up with all that rubbish."

"Oh, dear, I really don't know what I can do about that. Violet tends to take her position as housekeeper very seriously. I suppose I could have a word with her and ask her not to be quite so belligerent."

Polly grinned. "That's like asking Martin to do a tap dance while he's serving dinner."

"Yes, well, poor Martin is getting along in years, I'm afraid." Elizabeth sighed. "He used to be a very good butler. It's sad to see him so feeble now. Anyway, ring the Labour Exchange and see what you can do."

"Yes, m'm. I'll do that right away." Polly jumped up from her chair as Elizabeth rose to her feet. "I just want to say, Lady Elizabeth, that Violet's not all that bad. I got along with her most of the time. I liked being a housemaid, I really did, but I like being your assistant so much better."

"You're doing a wonderful job, Polly," Elizabeth assured her, with more generosity than the girl deserved. "Keep up the good work."

"Yes, m'm. Oh . . . there was one thing . . ." Her voice trailed off, and for once she looked unsure of herself. Although she was only sixteen, Polly normally had all the confidence and audacity of someone twice her age.

Elizabeth paused in the doorway. Polly's rail-thin body and straight black hair would have made her seem austere were it not for her huge, laughing brown eyes and ready smile. She wasn't smiling right now, however, and her troubled look unsettled Elizabeth. "Polly? What is it? Is something wrong? Your father?" Loved ones fighting overseas were always uppermost in her mind when she sensed problems with her staff.

"Oh, no, m'm. Me dad's fine. Least he was, last time he wrote. Doesn't say much in his letters, of course. You know what they say." Polly placed a finger over her lips. "Loose lips sink ships."

"Quite. So, what was it you wanted to tell me?"

"Oh, right. Well, it's them ghosts Martin is always talking about."

Elizabeth raised her eyebrows. "Martin? Polly, I thought you understood that we can't attach too much importance to anything Martin might say. He is, after all, well into his eighties. It's hardly surprising that he gets . . . confused at times. We must all do our best to let him think he's still useful, but I'm afraid his mind wanders quite a bit at times."

"Yes, m'm. I do know he flips out now and then. But this time I think he might be right about the ghosts. I saw them."

In spite of herself, Elizabeth felt a chill. Normally she ignored her butler's occasional bouts of senility. Martin had been with the family since before the turn of the century. He was entitled to "flip out" now and then, as Polly so succinctly put it. There was something in her assistant's eyes, however, that made her ask sharply, "Whatever do you mean?"

Polly looked down at her feet. She was wearing those thick platform shoes that the young girls liked so much. Elizabeth often wondered how she could totter around on them all day without breaking an ankle. "I saw them, Lady Elizabeth. There were three of them. Children, they were. They flitted across the great hall by the east wing."

Elizabeth let out her breath. Ever since the officers from the nearby American air base had been billeted in the east wing, life at the Manor House had not been the same. It was wartime, of course, and one had to make sacrifices. Nevertheless, there were times when she couldn't help longing for days before the war, when her parents were alive and the Manor House was bustling with visitors and had a full staff to take care of them. Things were so much simpler then.

Now she not only had American servicemen to worry about, there were all the problems of running the estate, made a hundred times worse by mounting debts, thanks to her ex-husband, who had gambled away her inheritance. The last thing she needed was her office assistant seeing ghosts.

"I really do think you might have imagined it," she said firmly. "I've done the very same thing myself. A shadow cast by the wind in the branches of a tree, a draft of cool air stirring the curtains, a cloud passing over the sun—when you're alone in the great hall with all those old portraits and ancient relics lying about, not to mention a full suit of armor, it's really not surprising you imagine a ghost or two."

"Three," Polly said, with disturbing conviction. "I saw three of them, your ladyship. I swear it. Floating across the great hall, they were."

"Are you quite sure it wasn't American officers creeping back to their rooms in order not to disturb the others?"

"It were the middle of the morning, m'm. They were

all gone, flying across the Channel, more'n likely."

"Quite." Elizabeth glanced at the ornate clock on the mantelpiece. "Well, let me know if you see them again. And please ring the Labour Exchange. Violet is getting extremely upset by all the extra work put upon her lately."

"Yes, m'm." Polly plopped down on her chair and reached for the telephone.

Leaving her to her task, Elizabeth headed for the kitchen.

Violet, her housekeeper, was the only able-bodied member of the original staff to remain at the manor, since one could not, in all honesty, include Martin in that category. Still, he tried his best, and when his best was sadly lacking, which was a great deal of the time, Elizabeth and Violet surreptitiously took over his duties, thus assuring the old man of his continued usefulness in the household.

If at times Elizabeth suspected that Martin was aware of his limitations, neither of them cared to speak of it. Martin represented the old school, life as it was before the war changed everything, and neither he nor the lady of the manor had any desire to give up the last shreds of a lost era.

When Elizabeth entered the roomy kitchen, Violet was stooped over the sturdy table, busily chopping thick red stalks of rhubarb.

"Thought I'd make a pie," she said when Elizabeth sat down opposite her. "We haven't had rhubarb crumble in ages. I got some extra lard from the grocer's. Percy's usually got some tucked under the counter."

"I hope he's not getting it from the American base." Elizabeth reached for the newspaper. "You know how I disapprove of all this black market nonsense. Percy is in danger of losing his grocer's shop if he keeps taking these risks."

Violet tutted. "Get out of bed the wrong side this morning, did we? What's bothering you, Lizzie? Had a tiff with Major Monroe, have we?"

Elizabeth looked up sharply. Since Violet had practically raised her, she was the only person in the world allowed to use the childhood name. That wasn't what bothered Elizabeth, however. Her friendship with the handsome American major, Earl Monroe, was very dear to her, a precious and delicate thing to be treasured, and she resented Violet's teasing.

"For your information, I haven't seen Earl in the last two days. Not that it's any of your business."

"Ah, so that's what's eating you." Violet looked smug as she piled the pieces of rhubarb into a large bowl.

A tangy fragrance drifted across the table, reminding Elizabeth that she'd had only a small bowl of soup for lunch. Since the rationing, meals at the Manor House had become rather meager, except for the rare occasion when Violet managed to acquire an extra pork chop or an egg or two. Elizabeth usually kept quiet at such times, mindful of the upheaval caused the time she'd discovered that Percy was dealing in black market goods. A still tongue in a wise head seemed the best policy these days.

Until now, anyway, which no doubt was why Violet watched her with her sharp eyes, her head tilted to one side in a way that always reminded Elizabeth of an inquisitive sparrow.

"Earl's absence is not what's bothering me," she declared, not quite truthfully. It always disappointed her when she didn't see him, at the very least for a brief greeting before he rushed off to the base, or arrived back, exhausted, after a mission.

Always there was the nagging worry that this time he wouldn't come back. So many of them didn't come back. She couldn't imagine how she would feel if he were one of them.

The fact that Earl had a wife and children waiting for him in America added guilt to her conflicting emotions about their relationship. Not that he had betrayed his marriage in any way. Earl Monroe was, and always had been, the perfect gentleman.

It was her own feelings for him, despite her best efforts

to ignore them, that prompted her guilt. Her only comfort was in knowing that he had no knowledge of her fondness for him, other than the friendship she valued so highly.

"So, are you going to tell me what's putting that scowl on your face, or are you going to sit daydreaming all day?"

Elizabeth dragged her thoughts away from Major Monroe. "It's this business of finding a new housemaid," she said, laying the newspaper down. "There was a time when one could find any number of young girls on the estate who were anxious to work at the Manor House. Nowadays they're all flocking to London, taking over the men's jobs for three times the money they can earn in service."

"And dodging the bombs while they do it," Violet muttered. "Blooming idiots, the lot of them, if you ask me."

"Most of them find that exciting."

"They wouldn't if they'd lost two parents blown to bits by a bomb, like you did."

"People don't think about things like that these days. War does strange things to people. They accept the fact that each day could be their last. They take risks and live each moment to the fullest, doing things they'd never do in peacetime."

Violet sniffed. "Wars don't last forever. One day the men will come back, and they'll want their jobs. It'll be hard on all those women to get on with their lives after that."

"It will, indeed." Elizabeth didn't like to dwell on such things. She hated the thought that the old life had gone forever, and nothing would ever be the same again.

"So what are you going to do about getting a new housemaid, then? I could really use the help. My old bones aren't what they used to be, and Martin's no blinking help."

"I've told Polly to call the London Labour Exchange. The assistant there told me there were plenty of young girls who would jump at the chance to get out of the city."

"Especially with the American air base on the doorstep," Violet said dryly. She picked up the kettle and filled it with water.

"Well, she did mention that, too," Elizabeth admitted. Deciding to change the subject, she reached for the newspaper again. "I can't believe that John Rickett has died. He wasn't that old. It says in his obituary that he was fifty-four. Why, that's younger than you."

"Don't remind me." Violet carried the kettle to the stove. "Have you found anyone to take over his plot in the Victory Garden?"

"Polly said her mother would like it."

"Well, I hope she's a bit more industrious than her daughter. The girl would do murder to get out of working, I swear she would."

"I'm sure Edna will take very good care of the plot." Elizabeth turned the page back to the national news. "I see Mr. Churchill will be giving one of his speeches to-night. We must remember to listen. So inspiring, that man. I really don't think the Londoners could possibly have held up this long without him."

Violet, who had disappeared for a moment, emerged from the pantry. "That's funny." She scratched her head with a bony finger. "I could have sworn I left the cheese in there."

Elizabeth watched her hurry over to the cupboards and open one.

"It's not here, neither." Violet spun around and dug her fists into her hips. "I bet that Martin's been in there. He loves cheese. I'll have his kidneys for stew if he took it."

"I'm sure Martin wouldn't do such a thing," Elizabeth said, feeling uncomfortable. One never knew these days exactly what Martin was capable of doing. "Where is he, anyway? I haven't seem him since breakfast."

"I don't know," Violet said grimly. "But you can be sure I'll find him."

Elizabeth rose from the chair. "Well, don't be too hard on him. He isn't himself these days."

"Gawd knows who he is, then," Violet muttered.

Elizabeth paused at the door. "I'm going to run down to the village. We have a tenant who's behind on his rent."

"Just watch yourself on that motorcycle. Them Yanks still haven't learned how to drive on the proper side of the road."

Elizabeth smiled. Sometimes her housekeeper sounded more like a mother. "I'll be careful."

"Your mother would turn in her grave if she knew you were tearing around the village on that machine."

"Very likely," Elizabeth agreed. "But we can't afford a car, and it's faster than walking." She closed the door before Violet could argue the point.

"Ew, Ma, why do I have to help you with the gardening tonight?" Polly wailed. "I was going to wash me hair."

Edna Barnett stood in the middle of her tiny kitchen and folded her arms. "Because I said so, that's why. Tell Marlene she has to help as well. With three of us out there, we can have it all done by the time it's dark. Thank goodness for double summertime, that's what I say. Now that we've put the clocks back two hours for the summer, it won't be dark until after ten o'clock."

"But I'm tired." Polly slumped on a kitchen chair. "Marlene is, too. She's been on her feet all day working in the hairdresser's."

"She spends half her time in that shop sitting reading film magazines," Edna said sharply. "Go and tell her she has to help. Once we get the plot all weeded out, I can take care of it meself. John already did most of the planting. It would break his heart to see that garden looking the way it does."

Polly looked at her hands. "I'll get dirt in me fingernails, and then Lady Elizabeth will get cross with me. You know how she is. I have to look me best at all times. I'm a secretary, after all, not a blooming gardener."

"Do I have to remind you, my girl, that there's a war on? We all have to do our part. It's a small sacrifice compared to all those poor buggers being bombed out in London. Lady Elizabeth was good enough to give up some of her land for the gardens, and the least we can do is take care of a few vegetables. Now get up them stairs and tell that lazy sister of yours to get down here before I box both your ears."

Polly got wearily to her feet. Once Ma got her dander up, it didn't do to cross her. "All right, I'm going." She stomped up the stairs, muttering under her breath so Ma wouldn't hear her.

She found Marlene lying on her bed, reading a tattered copy of *Picture Show*. "I feel so sorry for poor Clark Gable," she said when Polly sank down beside her. "They say they had to stop filming his latest picture because he was in shock over losing his wife."

"Who was his wife, then?" Polly asked, only mildly interested. Since she'd met Sam Cutter, an American squadron leader billeted at the manor, she couldn't get excited about film stars. Sam filled her thoughts and her dreams, and her only aim in life was to marry him and go to America with him.

"Carole Lombard, that's who." Marlene rolled over on her side. "You know, the one what died in that plane crash last year? They say he hasn't been the same since—"

Edna's strident voice echoed up the narrow staircase and bounced off the walls. "Are you girls coming, or do I have to come up there and get you?"

"Ooh, crikey, I forgot." Polly jumped off the bed. "Ma wants us to help her weed the plot in the Victory Garden."

Marlene groaned. "Always something." She rolled off her side onto her feet. "Still, look at the bright side. You might get a chance to see Sam while you're there." She tossed her thick red hair back from her shoulders. "I wouldn't mind seeing some of the boys meself."

"I don't get to see much of them, and I'm there all the time." Polly trudged down the stairs ahead of her sister. "They're flying missions every day now. It gets real scary, it does, wondering if Sam's all right. Sometimes it's days

before I see him." She speeded up as Edna appeared at
the foot of the stairs. "We're coming."

A few minutes later the three of them wheeled along
the coast road on their bicycles. Marlene was determined
to make a race of it, and Polly had a hard time keeping
up with her. The wind whipped off the sea, tugging at the
pins that held her long, dark hair in a twist. One of these
days, she promised herself, she'd have Marlene cut it
short. Then she wouldn't have to worry about no more
pins.

Racing after Marlene up the long driveway to the
Manor House, she didn't realize they'd left Ma far behind
them until she'd climbed off her bicycle and thrown it
down on the grass.

Lady Elizabeth had donated a portion of her once pris-
tine lawn to the village for their Victory Gardens, and
now, at the height of summer, green shoots and thick
leaves sprouted from every inch of the plots. A few
women from the village were already hard at work, either
kneeling in the dirt or bending over their tasks.

Polly had no trouble spotting the plot that had belonged
to John Rickett. Instead of the orderly pattern of neat
rows, tall white and yellow weeds nodded their heads in
a tangle of stalks and spindly vines. "Ooh, 'eck," she said,
gazing gloomily at the mess. "That's going to take some
bloody doing."

"Better not let Ma hear you swear like that." Marlene
pulled on a pair of gardening gloves and unstrapped a hoe
from her bicycle. "Come on, let's get to it. You start digging up that end and I'll start at the other. We'll have it
half done by the time Ma gets here."

Polly dragged a spade from its harness. "Not blooming
likely. She's halfway up the drive already." She stepped
onto the edge of the dirt and aimed her spade. "Here, wait
a minute!" She poked a freshly turned mound of soil with
her foot. "It looks like someone started digging in here
already." She wrinkled her nose. "It don't half smell
'orrible, too."

Marlene, busily wielding the hoe at the other end of the plot, didn't even look up. "Probably someone dug in some horse dung."

"Well, I wish they'd waited until we'd finished weeding." Polly stuck the edge of the spade next to the mound and stepped on it. "It would have been—" She broke off as her spade struck something solid. "Blimey, what's this, then?" Grunting, she shifted the blade of the spade to get under whatever was blocking it.

Bent over the handle, her nose just a foot or two from the ground, she felt something give. She shoved her foot down hard on the blade, and the object shifted, breaking through the crumbling soil to the surface.

For a long moment Polly stared at the thing lying right at her feet. Something cold slammed into her stomach as she realized what it was.

The human hand lay lifeless in the dirt, the fingers drawn into a claw. Just below where the rest of the arm disappeared beneath the ground, a gold watch clung to a grimy wrist, winking at her in the glow of the evening sun.

Polly let out one shrill, penetrating scream, then twisted away and was violently sick.

CHAPTER

❀ 2 ❀

If there was one thing Elizabeth disliked about riding a motorcycle, it was the way the wind tended to dislodge her hat, despite its firm anchor of pins and elastic. Her bunched-up skirts were another cause for concern, though she was careful to arrange them in such a way that she remained within the boundaries of decorum.

One had to make sacrifices in wartime, true, but as her dear, departed mother had impressed upon her at every possible opportunity, to a Hartleigh, appearance was everything. Which meant a hat and a decent frock whenever she appeared in public.

The misfortunes of her ex-husband at the gambling tables had left her almost destitute, and the constant struggle to keep up at least a semblance of affluence became, at times, overwhelming. It was, however, crucial to maintain the standards expected of her.

The Manor House, and all it stood for, was a symbol

of continuity in a world gone mad. The mansion had stood on the hill overlooking the village of Sitting Marsh for more than three centuries, home to the Earls of Wellsborough and their families. The fact that, thanks to the untimely death of her parents, there was no longer an Earl of Wellsborough was bad enough. The villagers had been forced to accept not only a woman as their guardian and adviser, but a woman of doubtful heritage. Faced with the formidable task of proving her worth, Elizabeth fought to keep up the traditions so long revered by her tenants. It wasn't easy.

Right now, she was struggling to hold onto her hat with one hand while maintaining a reasonable control over her motorcycle as she sped downhill toward the rows of cottages. Luckily she had a sidecar to help her balance— without it she would have had a great deal more trouble.

In spite of everything, she rather enjoyed riding the motorcycle. She usually caused a stir when she roared into the High Street, and it was important to make an entrance, no matter where one happened to be. Most of all, flying down the hill in this manner gave her a wonderful sense of freedom, in a way that would not have been possible inside an automobile.

Arriving at Sandhill Lane, she parked the motorcycle against the stone wall that separated the cottages from the road. Fred Bickham's cottage was at the far end of the row, and Elizabeth picked her way along the rutted path to the door, her mind dwelling on the matter of her new housemaid and wondering if Polly had rung the Labour Exchange before leaving for the day.

Thick black curtains covered the windows of Fred's cottage. Elizabeth frowned. It wouldn't be dark for at least another two hours. Most people waited until the last minute to draw their blackout curtains, holding on to every second of daylight they could. She lifted the door knocker and let it fall.

Everything seemed unnaturally quiet. She could hear no sound from inside the cottage, and there was no sign of the tenants in the neighboring cottages. Rather belatedly she remembered Churchill's speech scheduled for that evening. No doubt everyone was inside listening to their radios.

Once more she knocked on the door and waited. After a moment or two she gave up. Either Fred had retired early for the night, or he couldn't hear her over the radio. Then again, he could be in the Tudor Arms, enjoying a late evening pint of ale.

Deciding that her discussion with him could wait, Elizabeth returned to her motorcycle. Now all she could think about was returning home as soon as possible, in the hopes of seeing Earl Monroe before he retired for the night. It had been entirely too long since she had enjoyed a friendly chat with the major.

Filled with guilty anticipation, Elizabeth soared back up the hill toward the mansion. Turning in to the long driveway, she glanced across the rolling lawn to the far slope that led down to the woods. It was there that she had designated half an acre of land for the Victory Gardens. The area was out of sight from the mansion windows, and far enough away to avoid being disturbed by the volunteer gardeners.

From that end of the driveway, however, she had a clear view of the plots. As she coasted between the trees, she caught sight of a knot of people clustered around one end. Her curiosity caught, she slowed the machine and came to a stop. Something was definitely going on over there. She shut off the engine, intending to walk across to find out if there was a problem. As the engine died away, the sound of someone crying drifted across the lawn on the evening breeze.

Worried now, Elizabeth hurried toward the small crowd, wondering what new calamity she was about to encounter. She had almost reached the group when one of the women turned her head. Elizabeth's spirits sank when she recognized Rita Crumm. "Here she is now,"

Rita declared, leaving Elizabeth in no doubt that the women had been talking about her.

Her feud with Rita had started shortly after she'd taken over the reins of the Manor House and its estate. Rita had made it abundantly clear that she considered Elizabeth unsuitable and unqualified for the role formerly held by her father. After all, Elizabeth's mother had been nothing but a lowly kitchen maid when the future Earl had married her, thus diluting considerably the noble blood of the Wellsborough heirs.

In her eagerness to convince the villagers that her opinion was valid, Rita constantly attempted to surpass Elizabeth's efforts at every opportunity. This more often than not manifested in bold and significantly ill-advised ventures under the guise of contributing to the war effort.

It was Elizabeth's considered opinion that Rita's aim was to win the war single-handedly, earning the undying gratitude of a beleaguered nation and putting down once and for all that common upstart calling herself the lady of the manor. It was also her considered opinion that Rita had taken on one of the plots for the sole purpose of spying on the Manor House and its occupants, which was uncharitable, to say the least. Particularly since Rita's Victory Garden outproduced everyone else's. Naturally.

"Do we have a problem here?" Elizabeth asked cautiously, as heads turned in her direction.

One woman separated herself from the group, and stepped forward. Elizabeth recognized Edna Barnett at the same moment she spotted Polly on the ground behind her. Polly's knees were hunched most unbecomingly under her chin, and she rocked back and forth, moaning and crying in quite an alarming manner.

"Whatever's the matter?" Elizabeth exclaimed, hurrying forward. "Did you cut yourself with the spade?" It appeared to be the most likely cause of Polly's behavior, since the spade apparently had been flung some distance from the plot.

Edna seemed to be having difficulty forming words.

Her mouth opened and closed, but no sound came forth. Her face looked drawn and ashen, and her eyes were wide with fear.

Much against her better judgment, Elizabeth turned to Rita Crumm for an explanation.

Rita, of course, had no trouble obliging. "There's a dead body in the garden," she announced, with obvious relish.

Suspecting some kind of macabre joke had been played on poor Polly, Elizabeth was not amused. "I should think that we all have better things to do with our time than play pranks on one another," she said, more tartly than she'd intended. "For one thing, considering everything that's going on in this country, it's in beastly poor taste."

Edna's shaky voice spoke from behind her. "It's not a prank, m'm. There really is a dead body. It's right there. Our Polly dug it up . . . ooh, I think I'm going to be sick."

Elizabeth froze to the spot. Her sense of duty insisted that she take a look and satisfy herself that the women were telling the truth. Her natural instincts urged her to run home and let the constables take care of it.

She could not, however, walk away from this group of women, all of whom were staring at her as if she could resurrect whoever might be buried in one of her vegetable plots, and leave Polly sobbing on the ground. Someone had to take charge.

Her legs felt as if they were encased in ice as she forced them to move. She saw a bundle of filthy rags lying among the weeds, and a brief glance confirmed the shocking news. It was, indeed, a dead body. She aimed a second glance at the face, and her stomach immediately revolted. The features were completely unrecognizable, smashed to a pulp like a slab of raw meat. "I think you should all go home," she said faintly, and prayed they all did so before she made a spectacle of herself. "I'll ring the constables."

"Who do you think it is, then?" Rita asked, her voice sharp with avid curiosity.

"I doubt if anyone can answer that question right now."

Elizabeth shuddered, unable to get the image out of her mind. "Please, Rita, take your friends home with you. No doubt as soon as the body is identified everyone will learn who he is." Gossip, as Elizabeth well knew, traveled like wildfire in the village. News like this would be a lightning strike.

Rita apparently agreed with her, for she rounded up her little entourage and led them to where their bicycles lay in a heap on the driveway.

Elizabeth bent over Polly and patted her trembling shoulders. "Go home with your mother," she said gently. "Have a nice cup of tea and take some aspirin. You'll soon feel better."

The buxom girl standing behind Polly reached down for her hand. "Come on, Pol," Marlene said, her voice unnaturally loud, "ups-a-daisy then."

Polly, still sobbing, scrambled to her feet.

"It's the shock," Edna said, looking as if she were about to faint. "She'll be all right when we get her home."

Elizabeth nodded in sympathy. "Do let me know if there's anything I can do."

"Thank you, your ladyship."

Her stomach churning uncomfortably, Elizabeth followed them as they stumbled over to their bicycles. She waited until they were all well down the driveway before restarting the engine of her motorcycle. A few moments later she pulled to a halt in front of the stables.

Desmond would put the motorcycle away, she assured herself. Her first order of business was to talk to Sid and George. It would take them a while to get out to the mansion. After that, she could have Violet make a pot of tea. Maybe a dash of brandy in it would help her stomach.

The ancient bell echoed through the depths of the halls when she tugged on the rope. She waited impatiently for Martin to open the door, and wished she'd gone to the back door, where she could have let herself in with a key.

One day, she vowed, she would have proper locks put on the massive front door instead of the heavy bolts and latches that secured it now. Her desire to hold on to as much of the original trappings of the mansion as possible was being swiftly outweighed by the need for more modern conveniences, particularly now that Martin had become so feeble in both mind and body.

The object of her thoughts apparently arrived on the other side of the door. Well-oiled bolts slid across, latches scraped up, and at last the door slowly opened.

It occurred to Elizabeth at that moment that should George and Gracie, her boisterous bloodhounds, escape to freedom, they would no doubt find their way to the vegetable plots. She shuddered to think what might happen when they spotted the grisly remains.

Instead of waiting for Martin's wrinkled face to appear, she bounded through the door, brushing heavily against her butler's arm in her haste.

He spun around, arms floundering, his feet sliding on the polished floor. " 'Pon my soul!" he exclaimed in his wavering voice. "Now where did that blessed door go?"

Thankful that the dogs were nowhere in sight, Elizabeth gasped an apology. "So sorry, Martin, but I'm in a dreadful hurry. Please tell Violet to put the kettle on. I'll be down in a tick."

As she sped up the stairs to her office, she heard him mumbling behind her.

"A tick? What kind of tick? Is that some kind of evening attire?"

Making a mental note to stop using Polly's modern idioms, Elizabeth hurried into her office and reached for the telephone. Her call went unanswered at the police station, and she replaced the receiver with a grunt of annoyance. Ever since George and Sid had been dragged out of retirement to replace the village constables now fighting abroad, law enforcement in Sitting Marsh had deteriorated considerably.

George did what he had to in order to get by, and Sid appeared to be there for the sole purpose of annoying him. Unfortunately, several years of retirement, plus the fact that neither of them cared to be gainfully employed again, made their efforts lackluster at best.

There was nothing for it, Elizabeth decided. She'd have to go down to George's house and report the find. The tea would have to wait.

She flew down the stairs again and along the hall to the kitchen stairs. The moment she burst through the door, the two dogs leaped to their feet, tails wagging and tongues hanging from their mouths.

Violet's frizzy gray hair appeared to be standing on end as she spun around from the stove. "Whatever's got into you?" she demanded. "What's your blinking hurry?"

"Can't explain now." Elizabeth panted, striving for breath. "I have to go into the village. Just don't let the dogs out until I get back. I'll tell you all about it then."

"What about the tea? I just made it."

"Sorry." Elizabeth waved a hand as she dived for the door. "I won't be long."

Her knees felt as if they had lead weights attached to them as she hurried back up the stairs to the main hall. It was times like these when she realized she was getting older. Not that thirty-one was all that old, but she wasn't twenty-one anymore.

Her world had changed unbelievably in a few short years.

The thought momentarily depressed her, but then, as she hurried across the courtyard on her way to the stables, her melancholy vanished in a wave of relief. A jeep was parked close to the back door. Climbing out of it was a familiar figure.

"Earl! How good to see you!" She pulled up, and lifted a nervous hand to straighten her hat. The brim was definitely lopsided.

"Evening, ma'am." He raised his hand in casual salute. "Nice to see you, too."

She drew close, forgetting her own concerns at the sight of deep lines at the corners of his mouth. "You must have been busy. I haven't seen you for a while."

"Things have been pretty hot lately." He grinned at her, making light of his words, but she could see no humor in his eyes.

She could imagine how awful it must be for him, sending his men out on missions and knowing that some of them would almost certainly not return. Her greatest fear for him was when he joined them on a mission, as he seemed to do more and more often these days. Sometimes, when she lay in the dark of a soundless night, the dread of hearing that he'd been shot down was almost too much to bear.

She tried, so often, to remind herself how much worse it must be for his wife and daughters, waiting in a far-off country with little word from him, never knowing what he was doing or if he was safe. At least she could see him now and then, and reassure herself.

It was poor consolation, however, when deep in her mind she knew there would come a time when she would have to let him go. When he would return to his life and his family, and she would never see him again.

"Why so glum?" He tipped his head to one side. "Bad news?"

As always, she pushed away all thoughts of tomorrow. This was today, or rather, tonight, and she had to make the most of every moment she could steal with him. Right now, however, she had more important matters to take care of.

"Terrible news, actually," she told him. "Polly found a dead body in the vegetable plot."

Earl stared blankly at her, as if trying to make sense of her words. "The dead body of what?"

Stated like that, she had to admit it did sound awfully bizarre. "A human being, I'm afraid. A man. Impossible to tell who it is, even if I knew him. His face has been pummeled quite badly. His own mother wouldn't recognize him now."

At the memory of it, a wave of nausea took her by

surprise. She swayed on her feet, and Earl reached out to grasp her arm.

"Hey, you okay? You'd better sit down."

She shook her head. "Can't. I have to report this to the constables. I mean, he's just lying. . . ." She waved a hand in the direction of the plot. To her dismay, a sob lodged in her throat, and she swallowed hard.

"You're going down to the village?"

She nodded, not trusting herself to speak.

"Not on that bike, I hope?"

Again she nodded.

Earl reached for the door of the jeep and pulled it open. "Hop in. I'll take you down there myself."

Finding her voice at last, Elizabeth hurried to protest. "Oh, no, you can't. You're much too tired. You need to rest while you can. I couldn't possibly—"

"Are you gonna quit yakking and get in, or do I have to pick you up and put you in there myself?" He raised an eyebrow at her, then added belatedly, "Your ladyship."

Much as the thought of being swept up in his arms appealed to her, she decided it would be far more prudent to do as he suggested and get in the jeep. Actually, his commanding manner rather took her breath away. Did wonders for settling her stomach. She scrambled into the passenger seat and tugged the narrow skirt of her frock over her knees.

"Hang on to your bonnet," Earl said, giving her hat a rather critical glance. Then they were off, roaring down the driveway at an alarming speed.

George's house was at the far end of the village. Actually, Sid's house was closer, but since George always took charge of a situation, while Sid merely looked helpful most of the time, George was the lesser of the evils.

Earl insisted on accompanying her to the door, and the two of them waited on the tiny porch for someone to answer the loud rap of the door knocker. "Is Polly okay?" Earl asked, as the wait dragged on for a minute or two.

Elizabeth thought that was awfully nice of him to ask.

Before she could answer, however, the door opened, and Millie, George's wife, peered out at them. "Oh, good heavens, it's you, your ladyship." She clutched the neck of her blue flannel dressing gown and seemed quite flustered. Even more so when she caught sight of Earl. "Oh, dear. Whatever's happened?"

Elizabeth did her best to give her an encouraging smile. "Is George here, Millie? I'm terribly sorry to bother him, but I need to speak to him for a moment."

"He's just finishing his supper, your ladyship. Would you like to come in for a minute?" She glanced nervously at Earl. "You, too, sir, if you'd like."

"Thank you." Elizabeth ducked under a tangle of ivy and stepped into the tiny parlor. Earl followed her and pulled his cap from his head.

"He's in the kitchen," Millie said, backing away. "I'll get him." She fled through the door and disappeared.

Moments later George's gruff voice could be heard from the kitchen. "What's she want?"

Millie's voice was a low, unintelligible murmur.

"Does she know I'm in the middle of me supper?"

Millie raised her voice in an audible shushing. Again she murmured something.

"All right, all right, I'm going. Keep your bloody hair on."

Earl raised an eyebrow and Elizabeth felt a quite insane urge to giggle.

Then George appeared in the doorway. "Lady Elizabeth, this is a nice surprise." He ambled into the room, giving Earl one of those peculiar, uneasy glances most of the villagers reserved for the Americans. "Evening."

Earl nodded.

Elizabeth decided not to waste time with niceties. "George, you have to come back to the Manor House with us. There's something you need to take a look at."

George looked pointedly at the clock on the mantelpiece. "Can it wait until the morning, your ladyship? I'm in the middle of me supper right now."

"No, it can't wait. George, there's a dead body in my Victory Garden."

George's eyes grew wide. "I beg your pardon, m'm?"

"I said, there's a dead body in my Victory Garden. Polly dug it up. It's a man. That's all I can tell you. His face . . ." All of a sudden the room seemed terribly warm.

"Look, buddy, I think you'd better go take a look," Earl said bluntly. "Bring the M.E. with you."

George stared vacantly at him. "M.E?"

"Medical examiner. Doctor. Whatever you guys use to check out a dead body."

George turned pale. "I'll give Dr. Sheridan a ring. He can take me up there in his motorcar. Perhaps you should take Lady Elizabeth home, Major."

At that moment Elizabeth was concentrating on taking very deep breaths. Finding her voice again, she said firmly, "I want to be there when Dr. Sheridan arrives."

George pulled himself up another half inch. "This is police business, your ladyship. I can't have anyone interfering."

"The body is in my Victory Garden. I have a right to know who he is and how he got there." And, she added silently, she wasn't going to rest until she discovered the answers to both those questions.

CHAPTER

❦ 3 ❦

Elizabeth stood with her back to the vegetable plots while the men examined the body. Dr. Sheridan had brought both George and Sid with him and, in spite of their protests, reinforced by Earl's suggestion that she wait in the house, Elizabeth had insisted on being present.

She had to admit she was terribly glad of Earl's comforting presence as she waited in the gathering darkness while the doctor did his gruesome work. The smell was really quite awful, even though she stood several yards upwind of the makeshift grave.

"I hope you're not getting yourself mixed up in this mess," Earl muttered. "Whoever killed that poor guy could still be lurking around somewhere. He won't take too kindly to someone poking around and asking questions about it."

"Probably not," Elizabeth agreed. "But he should have

thought about that before he buried his victim in my Victory Garden."

Thanks to the constables' discreet use of torches, she couldn't see the expression on his face, but she heard the wry amusement in his voice when he answered. "Guess he doesn't know you too well, or he'd have found somewhere else to hide the body."

She was saved from answering that when George's voice startled her.

"Well, we think we know who he is, your ladyship."

The grass had deadened his footsteps, so she hadn't heard him approach. She spun around, blinking in the beam of George's torch. His face looked greenish in the subdued glow. He wasn't wearing his helmet, and she could see beads of sweat traveling down his forehead from the round bald patch on his head.

Feeling sorry for him, she asked eagerly, "Is it one of the villagers?"

"Well, we can't say for sure, m'm. Not until he's been properly identified, so to speak, but Sid recognized the coat and the scarf the poor blighter wore around his neck. Also, there's a photograph of a dog in his pocket, among other things. Sid recognized that, too."

"So who is he, George?"

"Well, I can't really say right now, m'm—"

"Of course you can," Elizabeth said impatiently. "Don't be a bore, George. You know I'm going to find out sooner or later, so you might as well tell me now."

"Can't say until he's been identified proper like," George said, with irritating finality.

Just then Sid arrived out of the gloom and paused at George's elbow. "We'd better get down to Betty Stewart's house," he said. "She'll be wondering about her husband, poor sod. Doc says he'll take Reggie's body with him in the backseat. One of us will have to walk back to the village, unless you want to sit next to poor old Reggie?"

George had turned on Sid in a frantic attempt to shush

him. Having failed, he cuffed his partner's ear. "How many times have I told you to keep your blinking mouth shut?"

"Betty Stewart is one of my tenants," Elizabeth said, her heart going out to the poor woman. "It's my duty to come with you when you inform her that her husband has died so brutally."

"Lady Elizabeth—"

Earl murmured her name just as George said loudly, "That really won't be necessary, your ladyship."

"Excuse me, but I think it is quite necessary. You know how flustered you get when faced with a hysterical woman. Sid can go with the doctor in his car, and I'll take you down to Betty Stewart's house in my sidecar. That way nobody has to walk down to the village."

"That's very kind of you, your ladyship," George said, "but I wouldn't want to put you out—"

"Come along, George," Elizabeth said, losing patience entirely. "It's getting late, and I haven't had my supper yet. The sooner we get this over with, the better."

"Wait a minute." Earl stepped forward. "I don't think your ladyship should be driving that motorbike on these roads at night, without lights. I'll take you both down to the village in the jeep, and I'll bring you home again after we drop George off at his house."

She looked at him, knowing he couldn't see the gratitude in her eyes. "I couldn't possibly let you do that, Major," she murmured, just to be polite.

"Let's go." Ignoring her protest, he marched off, heading for the courtyard.

Elizabeth had to run to catch up with his long stride, leaving George straggling behind them. "This is really very good of you," she said between puffs, as they hurried across the grass together. "But I hate to take up your time when you badly need to rest."

"Just how much rest do you think I'd get, knowing you were careening around the countryside in the dark on that darn motorbike?"

Warmed by his concern, she had to remind herself that he was merely being polite. "I'll be just as quick as I can. I simply can't let George handle this by himself. He hasn't the slightest inkling of how to handle these situations. Most men don't."

"Uh-huh. And I guess that ravenous curiosity of yours has nothing whatsoever to do with it, right?"

She smiled. "Of course not."

"Yeah, and my father's the president of the United States."

She gaped at him. "Your father? What happened to Mr. Roosevelt?"

Earl sighed. "He's still president. It's just a figure of speech."

"I see." Elizabeth shook her head. "You Americans have an odd sense of humor."

They reached the courtyard, where the dark shapes of three jeeps sat side by side. Earl opened the door of the first one in line. "Hop in."

She scrambled in, tugging at her skirt to keep it from riding up. "We'd better wait for George," she said as the sound of the jeep's engine splintered the silence.

"I'll pick him up on the way, if I can find my way down without lights. This blackout stuff is a pain in the neck."

Elizabeth glanced up at the sky. "The moon will give us some light."

She was right. The pale glow of moonlight revealed George's burly figure standing at the edge of the lawn, waving frantically at them as they drew close.

"He probably thinks I'm going down to Mrs. Stewart's house without him," Elizabeth commented.

Earl chuckled. "Don't tell me you're not considering it."

"I might, if George weren't carrying the coat and scarf. Without those, we can't be sure that it is Reggie Stewart."

"Maybe it isn't."

"Well, we'll soon find out. The body must have been

there for a while. Which means that if it is Mr. Stewart, he's been missing for the last few days."

"Good point. But then why hasn't his wife reported him missing?"

Elizabeth folded her hands in her lap. "That's exactly what I'd like to know." She jerked forward as the jeep came to an abrupt halt in front of George.

He climbed into the backseat, muttering something under his breath that Elizabeth couldn't quite catch. Wisely, she decided not to ask him to repeat it. She waited until they were speeding down the hill before asking him, "Did Dr. Sheridan say how long he thought the body had been buried?"

"About a week, he reckoned," George said, apparently forgetting he wasn't supposed to be discussing police business. "All them maggots must have had a few days to make that much mess of his face."

Elizabeth's stomach started churning again. "Yes," she said hastily, "I suppose so. Although it seemed to me that his face had been severely beaten before he was buried."

"The doc reckons someone took something like a hammer to his face." George leaned forward and tapped Earl on the shoulder. " 'Ere, mate, we drive on the left side of the road in this country."

"Sorry." Earl swerved to the other side of the road. "Keep forgetting."

"Bloody amazing we don't have a really bad accident on these roads at night," George muttered. "Yanks driving on the wrong side without lights. Bloody miracle, that's what I call it." As if recalling with whom he was traveling, he added quickly, "Begging your pardon, your ladyship."

"That's all right, George" she said cheerfully. "I've often wondered myself how they miss each other."

"Sometimes we don't." Earl braked sharply, sending them all jerking forward. "You didn't tell me where this lady lives."

"Just down here at the end of this lane," Elizabeth said.

"The Stewarts haven't lived here very long. I don't know them too well."

"Hell of a way to get acquainted." Earl pulled up in front of the peaceful-looking cottage. "Guess this is it. Want me to come in?"

Elizabeth looked hopefully at George, who shrugged. "Why not? The more the merrier. Let 'em all come in, that's what I say." He heaved an exaggerated sigh. "Police business isn't what it used to be, that I do know."

"All things change in wartime, George," Elizabeth said as she accepted Earl's hand to help her down from the jeep.

"Don't I bloody know it!" Still grumbling under his breath, George walked through the empty space between two laurel hedges and trudged up the path to the front porch.

With Earl hovering at her side, Elizabeth waited while George rapped the door knocker. From somewhere inside the house a shrill barking erupted, followed by a woman's voice shouting an order. A loud yelp ended the barking, and there was silence for a moment or two, then the door opened just a crack.

"What do you want?" a harsh voice demanded.

"Police Constable Dalrymple here," George said pompously. "I would like to speak to Mrs. Betty Stewart, if you please."

"Don't you have any idea what the flipping time is?" The door opened a little wider. "If you're collecting for the war effort, I've already given up most of my saucepans. And they came and took my iron gate away. What more do I bloody have to give?"

George cleared his throat. "I'm not collecting nothing. In case you haven't noticed, I have Lady Elizabeth Hartleigh Compton here with me, and Major Earl Monroe of the United States Army Air Force."

"Bloody hell." The door opened wide to reveal a plump woman wearing a tattered dressing gown. Her muddy blond hair hung in two long plaits down her back, and remnants of bright red lipstick clung to her puffy lips. Catching sight of Elizabeth, she made a feeble attempt to smooth the wrinkles from her dressing gown, then tied the cord tighter around her thick waist. "Didn't see you there, your ladyship," she muttered. "Did I do something wrong? I paid the rent just last week."

"It's not about the rent, Mrs. Stewart," Elizabeth said, stepping up to George's side. "May we come in for just a minute?"

Betty Stewart cast a nervous glance over her shoulder. "Well, my house isn't all that tidy right now. Can't you tell me what's wrong out here?"

"Mrs. Stewart," George began, but Elizabeth forestalled him.

"We don't mind at all. We shan't be that long," she said briskly, and stepped purposefully forward until the other woman had to move back and allow her into the house.

"Lady Elizabeth—" George tried again, and this time it was Earl who interrupted him.

"We might as well go in, buddy. The lady is not going to take no for an answer."

"I suppose so." Obviously put out, George stepped into the cottage with Earl hot on his heels.

The house smelled of recently fried bacon, and the parlor looked surprisingly neat and tidy, despite Betty Stewart's apologies. Clean, freshly ironed curtains hung at the windows, and the table that separated a couch from a comfy armchair was free of clutter, except for a small lamp and a rather expensive-looking pipe nestling in an ebony stand.

On the mantelpiece a pair of heavy silver candlesticks caught Elizabeth's eye. They were obviously antique, and probably quite valuable. No doubt handed down from previous generations. She wondered if Betty Stewart was aware of their value. Most people weren't too knowledgeable about such things.

Betty acted as if she'd been invaded by a swarm of

bees. Her gaze flicked from Elizabeth to George to Earl, then over her shoulder and back again while she fiddled with the cord of her dressing gown. "I'd offer you a cup of tea," she said, all the fight fading from her voice, "but I'm out of tea and I don't have much milk. The rationing, you know . . ."

"It's quite all right, Mrs. Stewart," Elizabeth said gently. "We really don't have time to stop for tea."

"Betty. Please call me Betty, your ladyship. It's an honor to have you in my house. Indeed it is."

"Mrs. Stewart," George said loudly, "I'm afraid I might have some bad news—"

Elizabeth held up her hand. "Let me handle this, George." She turned to the woman, who was now watching the constable through half-closed eyes. "Betty, is your husband home?"

Betty's eyelids snapped up. "Reggie? What's he got to do with this? Is he in some kind of trouble?"

"Is he home?" Elizabeth persisted.

Betty's chin came up in an expression of pure defiance. "No, he's not, Lady Elizabeth. Reggie left last week to join the Army. I haven't heard from him since." She didn't say the words, but her tone clearly indicated that her husband's lack of communication did not bother her in the least.

"I see," Elizabeth murmured. "Exactly when did you last see your husband?"

"Er . . . if you don't mind, I'm supposed to be the one asking the questions." George stepped forward. "Lady Elizabeth, this is police business. It has to be conducted by an official member of the constabulary."

Elizabeth gave in. "Very well, George. Get on with it."

"Yes, m'm. Thank you, m'm." George touched his forehead with his fingers, then turned back to Betty. "Mrs. Stewart, exactly when did you last see your husband?"

Betty rubbed her chin, and Elizabeth couldn't help noticing the tremor in her fingers. "It was a week ago last Saturday, that's when. He stormed out of the house and said he was going to join up. I tried to tell him he was too fat, and with his coughing all the time, they wouldn't take him, but they must have done, because he didn't come back. I don't know where he is now. He could be at the army camp in Beerstowe, I suppose."

"Mrs. Stewart." George cleared his throat. "I regret to inform you that Lady Elizabeth has discovered the body of a man buried on the property of the Manor House. We have reason to believe that the man is your husband, Reggie Stewart."

Betty stared at him, unblinking, for several seconds. The eerie silence was broken by the shrill bark of a dog somewhere in the house. Betty seemed to snap out of her trance. "Caesar! Shut up, do!" She glanced at Elizabeth. "Sorry, your ladyship. Strangers make him nervous. He doesn't like being shut up inside a room."

Earl, who had been quiet all this time, apparently was thinking the same thing that was on Elizabeth's mind. His voice rang with disbelief. "Excuse me, ma'am, but you did understand what the constable just said?"

"Yes, I did." Betty Stewart sounded completely unemotional.

"I have some of the victim's effects outside," George said, backing away. "I need you to identify them."

"All right." Betty waited until George had disappeared, then waved a hand at the comfortable couch. "I'm sorry, Lady Elizabeth, I don't know where my manners have gone. Please, sit down. You, too, Major."

Elizabeth sank onto the couch, while Earl waited for Betty to sit before choosing a deep armchair.

"I'm so sorry," Elizabeth said quietly. "This must all come as such a shock to you."

Betty looked down at her hands, still twisting the cord around her fingers. "Yes it is. That's if it *is* Reggie." She looked up. "Though you'd know him, I suppose, wouldn't you, Lady Elizabeth? You met him when we moved in here."

Thankfully, Elizabeth was spared from answering by

the return of the constable. He carried the bloodied coat and scarf over his arm, and Betty's gaze seemed riveted on them as he laid them on the arm of her chair. "Are these your husband's clothes?" he asked, stepping back.

Elizabeth held her breath as the other woman fingered the material of the coat, then let it drop. "Yes, they are," she said, her voice flat and lifeless.

George stuck his hand in his pocket and withdrew a creased photograph. "This is your dog?"

Betty glanced at the photograph and nodded.

"And I believe this belonged to your husband." George held out his hand, the gold watch dangling from his fingers.

Betty gazed at the gleaming wristband for a long moment, then took the watch from him. For the first time a tear squeezed out of her eye. "Thank you, Constable."

"I'm sorry, Mrs. Stewart."

She nodded, apparently overcome, though her voice was quite steady when she spoke again. "How did he die, Constable?"

"His head was bashed in," George said, with his usual total lack of tact. "That's why no one could recognize him. His face were a real mess, I can tell you."

"I think we've taken up enough of your time." Elizabeth rose to her feet and gave George a dark, meaningful glance.

"Quite, quite." George reached for the coat and scarf. "I have to take these in for evidence," he explained, as Betty seemed inclined to cling to them.

She released her hold on the clothes and got unsteadily to her feet. "Thank you for coming," she murmured.

"Will you be all right?" Elizabeth asked. "This isn't a good time to be alone."

"I'll manage." She managed a weary smile. "Thank you, Lady Elizabeth. It was kind of you to come."

Elizabeth studied the wan face. "I really don't like to leave you alone." It worried her that Betty showed so little emotion. She was very much afraid that when the truth finally penetrated, the poor woman could become hysterical.

"I prefer to be alone right now, your ladyship. But thank you, anyway."

"Very well, then. But if you should change your mind, please don't hesitate to send for me." She was about to head for the door when a soft thud caught her attention. The sound had come from the kitchen, where the door stood slightly ajar.

Betty must have noticed her glance over there, as she said quickly, "The dog. Always jumping on the furniture." She raised her voice. "Caesar! Lie down!"

A remarkably well-behaved dog, Elizabeth thought as she walked to the door. It clearly had access to the parlor, yet it hadn't bothered to investigate the visitors.

Outside, under a cloudless sky, she breathed in the perfumed air wafting from the night stocks that lined the pathway. The smell inside that house had been oppressive. Obviously Betty Stewart didn't believe in opening windows.

"Took that rather well, she did," George said, as the three of them stood by the jeep. "That was a big relief. I doubt my missus would be so calm if someone told her I were dead."

"I'm sure she would be devastated," Elizabeth murmured. "Then again, war does strange things to people. We see news accounts of all these young men injured and dying in the fields and on the beaches, women and children perishing in the ruins of their bombed houses, pilots shot down and horribly burned in their planes, and somehow, a man dying from a beating seems almost mundane."

She glanced up at Earl, whose facee seemed unusually grave. "Have we really become so hardened—so accustomed to violent death—that we have no compassion or respect for life anymore?"

"Gawd, I hope not," George muttered.

"Not you, Elizabeth," Earl said softly. "Never you."

Cheered by his words, she paid little heed for once to

the fact that he'd dropped her formal title—something he'd promised not to do in public. It didn't seem to matter right then. All that mattered in that moment was the sound of her name in that romantic American drawl that always stirred her blood. It was enough to chase away the demons of that dreadful evening, and give her hope that tomorrow would be a better day.

Earl didn't have much to say on the way back to the manor, and she was content to sit by his side with the fresh sea breeze cooling her face as they soared up the hill.

"Thank you for taking me down to the village," she said, when he pulled up in front of the mansion. "I really don't like riding my motorcycle in the dark."

"Anytime I'm free. All you have to do is ask."

She wished she could see his face more clearly. The shadows obscured his eyes, making it difficult to judge his thoughts. "Goodnight, Earl," she said quietly. "Please take care of yourself."

"Always." Thoroughly unsettling her, he reached for her hand in the dark and pressed it to his lips. "Goodnight, Elizabeth."

She scrambled out of the jeep before careless words could spill from her lips—words that might reveal her hopeless feelings. She heard the roar of the jeep's engine behind her as it took off toward the courtyard, but she resisted the temptation to watch it disappear.

Instead, she hurried past the steps leading to the front door and made her way past the greenhouses to the kitchen door. Although a brand-new lock had been installed at the outbreak of war, in response to the threat of an enemy invasion, it was rarely used. It was just too inconvenient for the tradesmen when they called. The milkman, for instance, put the milk directly in the pantry during the summer, so that it would stay cool.

The door opened on well-oiled hinges, and only the faint glow from the grate of the coal-fired water heater lit the kitchen. As she stepped inside, Elizabeth thought she saw a movement on the opposite side of the spacious room—a flutter of skirts, a shadow moving swiftly in front of the door that led to the hallway.

Chills shivered down her back as she peered across the room in cold disbelief. Polly's voice drummed in her ears. *I seen them, Lady Elizabeth. Three of them. Children they were. They flitted across the great hall by the east wing.*

Ghosts. No, she didn't believe in ghosts. The back of her neck prickled as the door opened, and the shadow slipped through. She especially didn't believe, she assured herself, in ghosts who had to open a door to pass through it. It would seem that whoever had invaded her kitchen this late at night was solid flesh and blood. The question was, who was it?

CHAPTER

❈ 4 ❈

"You must have come home really late last night," Violet said the next day, her voice accusing as she carried the pot of steaming porridge from the stove to the kitchen table.

Seated in her usual chair facing the window, Elizabeth watched her housekeeper serve dollops of the gray, sticky mess into her bowl. "I'm getting awfully tired of eating porridge," she murmured.

"I'm getting awfully tired of cooking it." Violet dumped the rest of the mixture into Martin's bowl.

He sat there, staring gloomily at it for several seconds before saying, "This looks like wallpaper paste."

"In that case, either eat it or spread it over the flipping wall." Violet dropped the pot into the sink with a clang that jarred Elizabeth's teeth. "You can't be that hungry, anyway, seeing as how you polished off the rest of the pork pie last night."

Martin lifted his chin and peered at her over the top of his spectacles. "I most certainly did not. I don't care for pork pie. Never have."

"You ate it for dinner the other night."

"I tolerate it when there's nothing else. If I were to pilfer from the pantry, I'd much rather have a wedge of good aged cheddar."

"So that's where the cheese went! I blinking knew it was you."

Martin sniffed. "I haven't had a decent piece of cheese in months. That stuff you buy at the grocer's tastes like rubber. It sticks my teeth together. I have a devil of a job getting them out of my mouth."

"There's a war on," Violet reminded him. "It's all they have." She glanced at Elizabeth. "Must have been you that had the pork pie, then. I thought you might have had something to eat in the village."

"I didn't eat supper at all last night," Elizabeth admitted. "Which is why I'd like something better than porridge for my breakfast."

Violet stared at her in dismay. "You didn't eat supper? You shouldn't go to bed on an empty stomach. It's bad for you."

"I wasn't hungry." Elizabeth toyed with her spoon for a moment. There were things she had to tell them both, but she was reluctant to do so until they had finished eating.

"Where were you going in such a hurry, anyway?" Violet demanded. "I had a dreadful headache last night, so I went to bed early. Never heard you come in, I didn't."

"I was . . . visiting one of my tenants." Elizabeth watched Martin sprinkle sugar on his porridge. There was a time, she thought wistfully, when one wouldn't dream of putting anything but brown sugar on porridge. Of course, there was also a time when porridge was just the appetizer to breakfast, not the entire meal.

As if reading her thoughts, Violet said briskly, "Well, if you didn't have supper last night, you'd better have your egg this morning, instead of waiting until Sunday."

"Never mind. I'll fill up on toast."

"So who did you visit, then? Not someone really sick, I hope." Violet's expression changed. "Someone's husband died overseas?"

Elizabeth sighed. She might have known she couldn't avoid the subject for long. "Actually, someone's husband did die. Though not overseas. Our new tenant, Reginald Stewart, was found dead last night."

Violet paused in the act of placing the tea kettle on the stove. "The coalman? Go on! He just delivered our coal a week or two ago. What did he die of, then? He wasn't that old, was he?"

"Early forties, I believe." Elizabeth stirred milk into her porridge. "We're not really sure how he died. It was . . . hard to tell."

Something in her voice must have given her away, for Violet's brown eyes narrowed. "He didn't die in bed, then."

Elizabeth glanced at Martin, who seemed absorbed with his breakfast. "No, he didn't. Polly . . . sort of . . . dug him up in our Victory Gardens."

Violet smacked the kettle down with such force that the lid fell off and clattered on the floor. "Someone buried him in the vegetable plot? Who would do such a thing?"

"Well, I rather think that's what the police would like to know."

"That will give the potatoes a unique flavor," Martin said, with morbid relish.

Violet rolled her eyes toward the ceiling. "Trust him to think of his stomach first."

"He's right," Elizabeth said glumly. "We'll have to close down that plot."

"Why? It's not like anyone's going to know, is it? I mean, he couldn't have been there that long, could he? Poor old John Rickett hasn't been dead that long, and he'd have known if there was a dead body in his vegetables, I would think."

Elizabeth sent her a look that she immediately translated. Her scrawny shoulders lifted in a shrug. "Just a suggestion." She bent over to pick up the lid of the kettle, and sounded breathless when she straightened. "Poor Polly. What a dreadful thing for her to find. How did his wife take it, poor bugger? Must have been a shock to her."

"You'd think so, wouldn't you?" Elizabeth murmured. "All things considered, she was remarkably calm. I suppose we are all becoming immune to violence and sudden death these days."

Martin lifted his head. "Sad state of affairs, madam. I was just telling your father this morning—"

"Don't start that again, you silly old fool." Violet lit the gas jet under the kettle. "You and your blinking ghosts. You know very well the master is dead."

"He'd be very upset to hear that." Martin finished the last of his porridge. "He looked the picture of health when I left him this morning."

"Blown to bits by a bomb," Violet said deliberately. "Him and Lady Wellsborough both. Nothing left of them to be a ghost, so you couldn't have seen him." She glanced at Elizabeth. "Sorry, Lizzie. Sometimes you have to be cruel to be kind."

"Quite." Martin dabbed at his mouth with his serviette. "In which case I shall refrain from being kind. May I have your permission to leave the table, madam?"

Elizabeth nodded. "Of course, Martin."

"Thank you, madam. If I may say so, I still find it considerably awkward sharing meals at the kitchen table with your ladyship."

"Yes, Martin. I'm sorry about that." Her answer was purely automatic, for she had engaged in the familiar argument more times than she cared to count. All this talk of ghosts had reminded her of the incident in the kitchen last night.

When she'd thought about it upon wakening that morning, she'd decided it had to be her imagination, but now she wasn't so sure. She waited until Martin had shuffled at a snail's pace from the room, before asking casually, "Violet, did you say you had food missing from the pantry?"

"I don't know as how you'd call it missing." Violet poured boiling water into a large silver teapot. "I know darn well that Martin has been pinching stuff while my back is turned."

"Maybe not," Elizabeth murmured. "There just might be another explanation for the missing food." Violet stared at her while she recounted her experience of the night before. "I couldn't swear to it, of course," she said, when she was finished. "It was awfully late and quite dark in here."

Violet shook her head. "I'd know if a stranger had broken into my kitchen."

"Not necessarily. It could have been one of the American officers looking for a late supper. Except. . . ." her voice trailed off as she concentrated on the fleeting memory.

"Except what?" Violet demanded sharply.

"Except I thought whoever it was wore a skirt."

"Blimey," Violet said, "you're getting as barmy as the old codger. Seeing things, you are."

"Thank you, Violet. That makes me feel considerably better."

"Sorry, Lizzie, but all this talk of dead bodies in the gardens and ghosts in the kitchen. . . . Seems to me you're letting things get you down. You have to keep a stiff upper lip and all that. Can't let the war get us down. Like Churchill says, blood, sweat, and tears, but we'll never surrender. Or something like that."

Elizabeth smiled. "You're right, Violet. I probably imagined it. It was, after all, a very long evening." She got up from the table. "Where are the dogs? I haven't seen them this morning."

"I shut them up in the stables. You told me not to let them out until you got back. You never got back, and I couldn't have them piddling all over the kitchen floor, so I put them out back."

"I'm sorry, Violet." Elizabeth hurried to the door. "I just didn't want them digging up the body and making things difficult for the constables. I'd have let them out when I came home last night if I'd known, but I didn't put my motorcycle away last night. I left it outside."

"I know," Violet said, tilting her head to one side. "I saw it. I thought you might have gone out with your major, seeing as how excited you were and all."

"He's not my major." Elizabeth turned away so that Violet couldn't see her expression. "Major Monroe was kind enough to give me a ride into the village, that's all."

"Uh-huh. There's more hanky-panky goes on in them jeeps than in all the bedrooms of Sitting Marsh put together."

Outraged, Elizabeth spun around. "Are you suggesting—"

"I'm not suggesting anything," Violet said calmly. "All I'm saying is that people gossip. Especially in a village the size of this one. I just think you should bear that in mind, that's all."

She should be angry, Elizabeth thought wryly. Except that Violet was right. She had an image to uphold, and there were certain people just waiting for her to compromise herself. "I'll keep it in mind," she promised. "I'm going down to the village this morning, after I've talked to Polly. I'd like to talk to Betty Stewart again, without the constables hovering over us."

Violet narrowed her eyes. "Since her husband was found buried on the manor grounds, I imagine he didn't get there by himself. Which means someone killed him."

"It rather looks that way," Elizabeth admitted.

"Be careful, Lizzie. I wouldn't want to see you mixed up in murder again. You almost got killed the last time."

"I'll be careful." Touched by her housekeeper's concern, she smiled at her. "I promise I'll be back in time for lunch."

"Good. I've got a nice stew and rhubarb pie."

Hungry already, Elizabeth left the kitchen and headed for the office.

She found Polly already there, looking a trifle pale but otherwise her usual exuberant self. "Can I have some time off this afternoon, your ladyship?" she asked, as soon as Elizabeth walked in the room. "Sam's on leave, and he wants to take me to Yarmouth."

Elizabeth glanced at the clock. "Did you call the Labour Exchange in London yesterday?"

"Yes, I did, m'm. They're sending three girls down this afternoon. I made a list of their names and everything." She waved a slip of paper in the air. "They'll be coming down on the bus, so they can walk up from Muggins Corner. I rang the Tudor Arms so they'll have a place to stay tonight. They can catch the bus back in the morning."

"I suppose we should find room for them here," Elizabeth said, half to herself. "That will give us time to observe them all and help us decide which one will work best for us."

"Yes, m'm. Shall I ring the Tudor Arms again and tell them to forget the rooms, then?"

"Yes, do that, Polly. I'll let Violet know we'll have three extra for supper tonight."

Elizabeth turned to leave, then paused as Polly asked tentatively, "Your ladyship? About me leaving early?"

"Oh, yes, I nearly forgot. You can have the rest of the day, Polly. Just be here bright and early in the morning."

"Oh, thank you, m'm!" Polly bounced off her chair, and for a moment Elizabeth thought the girl was going to hug her. "I'll be here early tomorrow, I promise."

"Well, have a good time." As Polly rushed off, Elizabeth wondered if she should have cautioned the child to behave, then decided that should be her mother's job. It occurred to her that Edna might not even know Polly intended spending the day with a man almost ten years her senior. For a moment or two she wrestled with her conscience, then let the matter go. It was wartime, after all.

Twenty minutes later, after having enjoyed a brief romp with the dogs on the lawn, she was on her way down the hill to the village.

Much to her disappointment, Betty Stewart was not at home when she knocked on her door. Elizabeth waited a few moments just in case she had caught the woman at an inopportune moment, but after a minute or two of silence, she gave up. Her conversation with the recent widow would have to wait until later.

She was about to ease her leg over the saddle of her motorbike when a thin, high-pitched voice called her name. Turning, she saw the gaunt figure of Joan Plumstone hurrying down the garden path of the cottage next to the Stewart house.

Elizabeth did not particularly care for Joan. For one thing, she was a staunch friend of Rita Crumm—her second-in-command, so to speak. Joan was also an avid gossip, with a penchant for embroidering the truth if the facts fell short of the desired drama. Elizabeth did her best to avoid the woman whenever possible.

Evidently that would not be possible today. Joan had already reached her garden gate and had pulled it open. "Lady Elizabeth," she called out in her penetrating falsetto, "could I have a word with you, please?"

Elizabeth reluctantly turned to face the woman and offered a desultory greeting.

"Your ladyship." Joan came to a halt in front of her. "I was wondering if you've seen Rita yet? She wanted to ask you if you'd be available to help out at the summer fete this year."

Elizabeth did her best to sound interested. "Please tell her I'll be happy to do what I can."

She turned to leave, but was prevented from doing so when Joan stepped between her and her motorcycle. "Oh, I'm sure there's a great deal that you can do, Lady Elizabeth. We'll need someone to give out the prizes, of course, and judge the dance competition and the baby pageant. We're planning a dog contest as well, so we'll need judges for that. Perhaps you and that nice major I see you with all the time?"

The gleam in her eyes made Elizabeth long to poke her in one of them. Or both. There were definite disadvantages to having to watch one's image. "I'll see what can be arranged," she said coolly. "It's this Saturday, isn't it?"

"Yes, your ladyship. I know it's short notice, but we weren't sure if we were going to have the fete this year. What with the war going on, and all. Seemed a bit frivolous, if you know what I mean. But you know Rita. Gets her teeth into something and won't let go. She said it would be good for morale. Whatever that means. We've all been working really hard to get everything ready on time."

"Very well, I'll do my best to set some time aside for the event."

"And the major?"

Elizabeth frowned, although Joan's face was the picture of innocence. "I'll mention it to him." She paused, then added deliberately, "If I should run into him."

"Thank you, your ladyship."

"Not at all." Elizabeth waited for the woman to step aside, but Joan seemed determined to hold her ground.

"I couldn't help noticing you and the constable in Betty's house last night," she said, leaving Elizabeth in no doubt as to the real reason she'd confronted her that morning. "Has something happened to Reggie?"

About to pretend ignorance, Elizabeth thought better of it. "What makes you think something happened to him?" she asked, hoping she sounded indifferent.

Joan looked over her shoulder as if afraid of being overheard. "Well, I haven't seen him around for a while. Betty told me he'd gone in the army. Can't see as how they'd take him, though. Got too much weight on his middle and always coughing. Can't be too healthy, if you ask me."

Thoroughly interested in spite of her reservations, Elizabeth prompted another response. "It does sound as if he might have been turned down."

"Well, and then there's his drinking. Hardly ever seen him sober, I haven't. His liver must be shriveled up like a prune. Drinks like a fish, and temper to go with it. I don't think he ever has a bath, neither. The dirt's just grimed into his skin. Sometimes he looks just like a black man from Africa."

"Well, he did deliver coal for a living." For some reason, Elizabeth felt compelled to defend the poor man. No matter what he was like, he certainly hadn't deserved to have his face smashed to bits.

Joan was sharper than Elizabeth realized. "Did?" Flushed with anticipation, she lowered her voice. "You mean he's *gorn*, then?"

Inwardly cursing her slip of the tongue, Elizabeth said hastily, "I'm afraid I really can't talk about it right now. Perhaps Mrs. Stewart can tell you more when she comes home."

"I just knew something bad was going to happen to him," Joan declared, once more effectively halting Elizabeth's escape. "I could see it coming."

"Oh?" Elizabeth tried to sound only mildly interested, but she doubted if Joan had even heard her. The woman couldn't wait to rattle off everything she knew.

"Used to argue something terrible, they did. The two of them. They had a dreadful row right out here on the street. Reggie was going on and on about Betty spending all her time at the bank. Accused her of making eyes at Henry, he did."

"Henry?"

Joan's voice had an edge to it. "Henry Fenworth, your ladyship. The manager at the bank in the High Street? Hasn't been there that long. Widower, he is. Nice-looking chap. Too young for Betty, I'd say. Then again, there's no accounting for taste. Don't know why he's not in the Army, though. Must have something wrong with him, I s'pose. Still, he's more Betty's type than that filthy drunk she married. Had to get married, she did. She was six months along at the wedding. Then she lost the baby. Never had another. Doesn't surprise me. I would never let filth like that touch me. I reckon he forced her the first time. Can't see her doing it otherwise. I think—"

Deciding it was high time she put a stop to this flow of gossip, Elizabeth said firmly, "Well, I really must be running along. Please tell Rita I shall do my best to help out at the fete."

"I will, m'm. Thank—"

The rest of the sentence was drowned out by the roar of Elizabeth's motorcycle. As she rode back up the hill, she went over everything that Joan Plumstone had told her. Perhaps it wouldn't hurt to pay a visit to the bank. She hadn't met the manager yet, and with her shaky finances, it might be a good idea to make his acquaintance. Besides, she couldn't help wondering just how much truth there was in Reggie Stewart's accusations.

Someone had brutally murdered Reggie, apparently in a fit of rage. Could a love triangle have been the motive? It was certainly worth investigating.

It would have to wait for a while, however. With Polly gone for the day, she had a golden opportunity to catch up on tasks in the office that had gone neglected lately. Polly was a great help, but she could be a very distracting presence at times.

At the very first opportunity, she promised herself, she'd run down to the bank and meet Henry Fenworth. Just to satisfy her curiosity, of course. After all, one couldn't expect the local constables to think of everything.

CHAPTER

❀ 5 ❀

Polly leaned her bicycle against the garden shed and hurried into the house. Ma would be out shopping most of the morning, and she wanted to make sure she was out of the house before Ma got back. Ma didn't know she had the day off and was going on a picnic at the seaside with Sam. She'd carry on something awful if she knew.

Polly opened cupboards, snatching whatever she could find for the picnic. Not that there was much to choose from. She took down a tin of sardines, started to put it back, then changed her mind and stuffed it inside her old school satchel, along with the bread and small square of cheese she'd found in the larder.

Two apples sat in a dish on the sideboard. They looked a bit wrinkled, but Polly grabbed them up and threw them in with the rest of the stuff. She found two bottles of cream soda in the cupboard over the sink, and emptied the tin of broken biscuits into a paper bag. Percy sold the broken ones off-ration, so she didn't feel so guilty taking them.

Heaving the heavy satchel over her shoulder, she rushed out of the house and started walking up the hill toward the Manor House. Sam had promised to come down in his jeep and fetch her. She didn't want him at the house when Ma got back from shopping. If Ma knew how she felt about Sam, she'd have kittens. She'd put a stop to her working at the manor, that was for sure.

The trouble was, Ma knew Sam was a lot older than her. What Ma didn't know was that Sam thought she was twenty-one, when really she'd only just turned sixteen. Sam was twenty-four, and would probably have nothing to do with her if he knew how old she really was.

Marlene kept saying she should tell him, but she wanted to wait until she was sure he was madly in love with her before she told him. One day she was going to marry him and go to America with him. Polly smiled blissfully as she indulged in her favorite daydream. A house in Hollywood near the sea, with a swimming pool and everything like she saw in the films at the cinema. A house just like the film stars lived in, that's the house she wanted. And Sam was going to get it for her. One day.

So absorbed was she in her dream, it was a shock when the star of her elaborate fantasy roared down the hill toward her.

As always, her first sight of Sam took her breath away. With his brown eyes and thick, dark hair, he was the most gorgeous man she'd ever set eyes on. But it was his voice that really sent her, a deep drawl that thrilled her to the bone.

She'd lie in bed at night, hearing his voice over and over in her mind. He'd kissed her only a few times, but she could remember every second his lips had touched hers, and the weird but exciting feelings she got whenever he was that close to her. Marlene kept warning her to watch herself with him. She told her shocking stories about what men did to young girls when they got heated up. But so far, Sam had been the perfect gentleman.

In fact, Polly thought wistfully as Sam pulled up beside her, she sort of wished he *would* try something. Not that she'd let him go all the way, of course. But it would be nice to know he wanted to.

"Hey, gorgeous!" Sam grinned down at her, flashing white teeth. "Looking for someone?"

She smiled happily back at him. "Go on with you. You know I was looking for you."

"Well, what are you waiting for, sugar? Hop right in." He patted the seat next to him, and held out his hand for the satchel as she swung it off her shoulder.

Seated next to him, she let the wind take her long black hair as they started off, enjoying the feel of it streaming behind her. "You know how to get to Yarmouth?" she asked, as they turned off at Muggins Corner.

"Sure. I checked it out on the map."

"Well, we're not going to get very far if you keep driving on the wrong side of the road."

"Oh, shit!" Sam swerved to the other side of the road. "Sorry. I do okay until we turn a corner."

She snuggled up to him, her face pressed against his shoulder. "I'll remind you." She took a deep breath through her nose. He smelled so good. English boys didn't smell half as good. She'd never smelled anything as good as Sam. He smelled like a bar of scented soap, only more manly.

"Got a present for you," he said, as they swept down the coast road. "In my pocket, right next to you."

Eagerly she reached into his pocket and pulled out a flat brown cellophane package. "This? What is it?"

"Open it."

She tore it open and peeked inside, then gasped as she pulled out the filmy, delicate fabric. "Stockings! They're so silky and thin. Are they silk?"

"Nylons. All the girls are wearing them Stateside."

"Nylons." She breathed the word, letting the fine material slip through her fingers. She'd heard the girls talk about them, of course, but this was the very first time she'd actually seen any. They were the most beautiful things she'd ever seen. She couldn't wait to find out how they felt on her legs.

"Thank you ever so much." She carefully slid them back into the package. "I don't wear stockings in the summer, but as soon as it gets cool enough, I'll put them on."

"Do I get to see them on you?"

Polly felt a quiver in her stomach. She'd heard something in his voice that sounded different—disturbing, somehow. "I'll have to think about it," she said lightly, but her mind was racing ahead, imagining herself strutting around with Sam staring at her legs in the filmy nylon stockings. She'd never let anyone see her suspender belt, let alone a man like Sam.

All of a sudden she felt nervous. She wasn't sure she liked the idea of him seeing that much. She didn't want things to change. She just hoped he wasn't going to spoil their day together by trying to do the things that Marlene kept telling her about. If he tried, she'd just have to tell him she was a nice girl and didn't do things like that with men. He'd understand.

She snuggled up to him once more, trying to recapture the heady feeling of moments ago. But somehow the sparkles of sunlight on the ocean didn't seem as bright as they had, and the salty wind felt a little cooler in her face. Although she couldn't say why, she felt sad inside, as if something were already lost and she knew she'd never find it again.

Elizabeth sat at her desk in the quiet office, sorting through a pile of letters that Polly had left for her. Mostly bills, she thought gloomily, as she pored over the scribbled statements. Somehow she would soon have to find a way to raise more money if she were to keep the Manor House running in good order.

Most of the minor repairs could be handled by herself, with the help of Violet and Desmond, whose position as gardener had kept getting stretched lately into handyman, electrician, plumber, chimney sweep, and anything else his limited skills could manage.

It was the really big jobs that needed more expertise than her household staff could handle. Like roof and chimney repairs, windows replaced, crumbling masonry restored. Not to mention the water system that needed replacing. Despite everyone's best efforts, the pipes still gurgled and groaned every time someone used the bathroom in the east wing.

Before the Americans moved in, that hadn't been much of a problem, but nowadays, with all that banging and teeth-grating screeching in the pipes, at times the great hall sounded like rush hour at Waterloo Station. No wonder poor Martin thought he saw the ghost of her father walking the halls. The noise was enough to waken the dead.

Thinking about Martin's ghosts reminded her of the shadow she'd seen in the kitchen the other night. It did seem that someone might be stealing food from the larder. Yet the only women in the house at that time of night were herself and Violet. Unless Violet was sleepwalking, the only other explanation seemed to be that one of the Americans had taken to wearing skirts. Or perhaps a nightshirt.

Preoccupied with the puzzle, Elizabeth slit open a small envelope with her father's gold-edged paper knife. The ebony handle felt smooth from years of use, and she ran her thumb over it before laying it down. Her parents had been gone three years now, and she still missed them dreadfully. Especially at times like these, when the problems of running the estate threatened to overwhelm her.

She withdrew the slip of paper from inside the envelope and unfolded it. Inscribed in a shaky hand, the words wandered across the page. Elizabeth squinted at the untidy scrawl. After a moment she realized the letter had been written by Fred Bickham. He was giving her notice that he was moving out of the cottage. He was going to Ireland, where he planned to live with his brother.

Elizabeth frowned. He still owed more than a month's rent. She'd have to get down there before he moved out if she wanted her money. She glanced at the clock. Still an hour before the midday meal. She just had time to pop down there on her motorcycle and talk to Fred.

Just in case, she hunted through a drawer until she found the box that held the keys to all her cottages. Sorting through them, she found the one labeled with Fred's name. Much as she liked Fred Bickham, if he thought he was going to scoot off to Ireland with her rent money in his pocket, he could think again.

Minutes later she was on her way down the hill to Fred's cottage. The blackout curtains still covered the windows, giving her a nasty feeling as she rapped loudly on the door. The feeling intensified while she waited for Fred to answer her knock.

Finally, she made the uncomfortable decision to inspect the cottage. Fred, she knew, suffered from a weak heart, which was why he hadn't been called up. He lived alone, his wife having died of pneumonia a few years ago. There was a strong possibility that she'd find him dead on the floor. The idea made her all the more reluctant to turn the key in the lock. Someone had to do it, however, and she might as well be the one, since she owned the cottage.

Very carefully, she pushed the door open. It was pitch black inside, and she left the door ajar as she stepped into the parlor. She wished now that she'd brought Violet with her to inspect the cottage. Or better yet, Earl Monroe. She never felt afraid or nervous when she was with the major. She could sense a tremendous inner strength in him that seemed to fill her whenever they were together. He made her feel fearless, confident that she could handle whatever life threw at her. No man had ever made her feel that way before.

Right now, however, Earl was somewhere in the skies over Germany, or France, or wherever the war had taken him, and she was alone in this musty, airless cottage where the silence seemed to hover all around her like a threatening cloud.

She stood for several seconds, heart beating wildly, and listened for a sound that might mean Fred was in the cottage somewhere. The silence grew even more oppressive, and she knew she would have to explore further.

Quickly, she reached for the black curtains and drew them back, flooding the tiny room with sunlight. Dust lay in thick layers everywhere—it danced in the rays of the sun and settled on the clock on the mantelpiece, the candlesticks on the dining table, the radio on the sideboard, the crowded bookshelves in the corner.

Cobwebs hung from the ceiling, and one looped from the doorjamb to a lopsided picture frame. Obviously Fred was not the best housekeeper in the world.

Holding her breath, Elizabeth picked her way to the kitchen door and peered inside. Dirty dishes lay in the sink, and a pot half full of soup sat on the stove. If Fred had already gone to Ireland, he'd left in a big hurry.

Withdrawing her head, Elizabeth eyed the narrow staircase opposite the front door. The last thing in the world she wanted to do was go up those stairs. Convinced now that she'd find Fred dead in his bed, she was tempted to call in at the police station and ask George to investigate the bedrooms.

She turned toward the door, then reminded herself she was, after all, the lady of the manor. If she couldn't find the courage to look in on a helpless old man, then she didn't deserve the title. Squaring her shoulders, she slowly climbed the stairs. Each one snapped and creaked, jarring her nerves.

Reaching the top, she stepped onto the landing. In spite of the sunlight below, the shadows were thick and dark in the tiny hallway. Both bedroom doors were closed. After a moment's hesitation, she curled her fingers and rapped with her knuckles on the nearest door. "Fred? Are you in there? Are you all right? It's Lady Elizabeth. I came to see if you were all right."

In the silence that followed, she glanced at the second door. Deciding it couldn't hurt, she wrapped on that one, too. "Fred? It's Lady Elizabeth. Are you there?"

Nothing but silence greeted her efforts. Out of options, she reached for the handle of the first room and turned it. The hinges squeaked and she jumped, every nerve in her body tightening in dreaded anticipation.

Peering inside, she could see nothing in the black depths of the room. Blackout curtains covered the windows, with not even a chink of light filtering through. She opened the door wider and waited for her eyes to adjust. The room smelled like the public bar of the Tudor Arms—a damp, smoky, stagnant smell of spilt beer and stale cigars.

As the gloom gradually lightened, she could make out the bed. The covers were in a heap, the pillows were tossed to the foot, but there was no dead body lying on it.

Conscious of her shallow breathing, Elizabeth edged around the bed to the window. Her hand shook as she drew back the curtains and flooded the room with welcome light. Bracing herself, she turned, and her breath rushed out in a sigh of relief. The room was empty. If Fred had died, he hadn't done so in his bedroom.

Heartened by the fact, she threw open the door of the second room. It, too, was empty, except for two or three packing cases, a couple of boxes, and pages of torn newspaper strewn around. Obviously this was where Fred had done his packing.

As her heart steadied to its normal pace, Elizabeth felt like crying. It very much looked as if Fred had gone to Ireland, taking her rent money with him. Money that she depended on. Every penny of it. In view of all the bills sitting on her desk, this was a calamity that seemed to overwhelm all others.

Within seconds, however, her misery turned to anger. She would find out where Fred's brother lived and track him down. She was not going to accept defeat without a fight.

After she stomped back down the stairs, she eyed the various odds and ends about the place. Since Fred had seen fit to leave them behind, surely it wouldn't be considered improper for her to sell them. Discreetly, of course. But it might be difficult to sell a man's personal belongings with anything approaching discretion.

She wondered if he'd left any clothes in the wardrobe. She hadn't thought to look. At least she could give those to the clothes drive for bombed-out victims. Right now, however, all she could think about was getting out of the musty cottage and breathing some clean, fresh air.

The welcome sun warmed her face as she stepped outside, and she quickly closed the door and locked it. If she were to rent the cottage again, she'd have to get it cleaned. Polly had been responsible for that in the past, but now that her duties were more refined, she'd likely consider it beneath her to clean cottages. Especially one as filthy as this.

Immersed in her thoughts, she was startled to hear a jovial voice booming almost in her ear.

"Lady Elizabeth! 'Pon my soul, you're a welcome sight, I must say! What brings your ladyship down to our humble abode this fine morning?"

Elizabeth blinked, her gaze momentarily dazzled, until she recognized the neat white beard and twinkling blue eyes. "Good morning, Captain Carbunkle. How nice to see you again."

"Likewise, dear lady." The retired sea captain waved his pipe at her.

Elizabeth had never seen Wally without his pipe. As a member of the town council, he had contributed a great deal to the welfare of Sitting Marsh and its inhabitants. His experience and shrewd assessments had proved invaluable during her early days as administrator, and she would always be grateful to him. There were times, how-

ever, when she fervently wished that he'd leave his pipe
at home.

"I'm so glad to have bumped into you, Captain." She
tilted her head so that the brim of her blue straw hat
shaded her eyes. "I was calling on Fred, but he doesn't
seem to be at home. You don't happen to know where he
might be, I suppose?"

Wally poked his pipe into his mouth and took a couple
of puffs. "Now that I come to think about it, I haven't
seen Freddie in about a week. Must have been that long.
Last time I saw him was in the Tudor Arms. Saturday
night, it was. Having a grand old time, too, I can tell you.
He was playing darts with Reggie Stewart. They were
both drinking and smoking and carrying on, like they
were the best of pals. Surprised me to see them. I always
thought that Reggie bloke was a bit of a loner, if you
know what I mean."

His expression changed. "Strewth, Freddie was with
Reggie. Must have been about the same time he disap-
peared. I haven't seen either of them since that night.
Freddie might have been the last blinking bloke to see
Reggie alive. Makes you think, dunnit?"

"It certainly does," Elizabeth said gravely.

"Bad business, that. Any news on who might have
bumped the poor blighter off?"

The news, it seemed, had spread quickly on the grape-
vine, as usual. "None, I'm afraid. I wonder, Captain, did
Fred say anything to you about going to Ireland to live
with his brother?"

Wally looked puzzled. "Ireland? Freddie? Never mentioned anything like that to me. I didn't even know he
had a brother."

"Well, thank you, Captain. I really should be running
along."

"Right you are, your ladyship. See you at the next
council meeting?"

"Yes, of course. We'll have the proceeds of the annual

garden fete by then, so we shall have plenty of business to discuss."

"Right. Will you be going to the fete?"

"I expect so. I hope to see you there."

"Wouldn't miss it, your ladyship."

"Thank you, Captain." Leaving him with a smile, Elizabeth hurried back down the path to where she had left her motorcycle. Now she had more than one reason to find out where Fred had gone. If he had, indeed, been the last person to see Reggie alive, he might very well be able to shed some light on the mystery.

It was time she spoke to the constables. With their resources they'd have a much better chance of finding Fred than she would, and now she had a legitimate excuse.

Since she had to pass the police station on her way back to the manor, it seemed a good idea to stop in on her way back. As she rode down the High Street, she had a clear view of the building. Though she was still some distance away, she recognized the woman who hurried down the steps of the police station. She paused for a moment, looking up and down the street, then disappeared through the doors of the bank that stood next to it.

There could be only one reason Betty Stewart would visit the police station. There had to be developments in the case of her husband's murder. In which case, Elizabeth decided, it was up to her to find out exactly what those developments might be.

CHAPTER

❧ 6 ❧

It took Elizabeth a few minutes to reach the police station and park her motorcycle next to the bicycle rack. Peering through the glass-fronted door, she could see no sign of George or his befuddled partner, Sid, at the front desk.

A bell jangled loudly as she pushed the door open, and a voice from a room in the back roared, "Who is it?"

"It's Lady Elizabeth." She let the door swing to and crossed the room to the desk. "I'd like to have a word with you, George."

"Just a mo', m'm. I'll be right there."

She heard a scraping of chair legs on bare floorboards and a muttered exclamation before George's round, balding head appeared around the doorway. "Morning, your ladyship." The rest of him followed, one hand clutching the remains of what appeared to be a thick ham sandwich. "Just having me lunch, I was. What can I do for you, then?"

Elizabeth came straight to the point. "You can tell me what Betty Stewart was doing in here."

George's face seemed to close up. "Now, your ladyship, you know very well that's police business. I'm not at liberty to say. Can I offer you a chair?"

Sighing, Elizabeth sat down. This was a game she was well used to playing. All the same, she resented having to indulge George's irritating insistence on sticking to protocol when he knew perfectly well that she would ferret out the truth eventually.

"I assume that Mrs. Stewart's visit had something to do with her husband's murder," she said, folding her hands over her handbag.

George looked blankly at her.

Sid's grating voice wafted from the back room. "Can't assume nothing, your ladyship."

"Shut up, Sid," George growled.

Sid's lowered voice could be heard muttering something unintelligible.

"Does that mean she wasn't here about her husband's murder?" Elizabeth demanded.

George shrugged, but offered no comment.

Elizabeth thinned her lips. "I ask that you at least give me the courtesy of an answer when I ask a question, George."

"Yes, m'm. It's just that my lips are sealed, so to speak."

"Then nod, or shake your head. After all, you've done so plenty of times before."

George looked as if he were about to explode. His cheeks got very red and puffed out, and for a moment Elizabeth was quite alarmed, thinking he might be about to have a stroke.

Then his breath came out in a violent burst. "Begging your pardon, your ladyship, but every time I tell you what I know, you go charging off into police business and get into all sorts of trouble. The inspector's got wind of it, and he isn't too happy with me right now."

"I'm sorry, George." Elizabeth conjured up her sweetest smile. "I promise I won't get into trouble this time. I would just like to know why Betty Stewart was here, that's all."

"She was robbed!" Sid called from the back room.

"Sid!" George howled.

Elizabeth raised her eyebrows. It wasn't the answer she was expecting. "Robbed? Someone broke into her house?"

George rubbed his eyes with stubby fingers. "All right, if you must know, your ladyship. Someone got into her house last night while she was out. I'll be going down there right after I finish me lunch." He gestured with his half-eaten sandwich. "Until then, I don't know no more than you do. That's the truth."

Elizabeth turned the news over in her mind. "Did she say what was taken?"

"The usual stuff—clothes, money, food—"

"Food?"

George gave his sandwich a fond glance. "Just about wiped her out of her week's rations, she said. She was going to see Percy in the hopes he could help her out with a little bit under the counter, if you get my meaning."

But she didn't, Elizabeth thought. Betty Stewart had gone straight to the bank. Of course, she could have gone there to get some money. Then again, if she were upset, she could have gone to someone for comfort. Like Henry Fenworth.

"These days," George said, still gazing at his sandwich, "it's a bloody disgrace to steal food, what with the rationing and all."

"It is, indeed," Elizabeth agreed. "George, I think we might have a problem here. Violet has been complaining about food missing from the larder. She thought it was Martin, but the other night I could swear I saw someone slip out of the kitchen when I got home. I'm wondering now if we have a thief going around the village stealing food."

George sat down rather heavily behind the desk. "Gawd, where's it going to end? What with a murderer and now a robber lurking around the village, Sitting Marsh is becoming as evil as London, I swear it is."

"Speaking of which, how is the murder investigation going? Anything new? Has the murder weapon been found yet?"

George sighed. "Even if it had, your ladyship, you know very well I couldn't discuss it with you. But so far, we haven't found any weapon. We don't even know how Reggie died for certain. The doctor seems to think he died of a heart attack, probably brought on by the beating he took. But as to who beat him up, we've got no idea. It's going to be hard to find out now, seeing as how he's been in the ground for more than a week. Whoever did it is more than likely miles away by now."

"Unless the thief and the murderer are the same person," Elizabeth said quietly. "Perhaps Mr. Stewart saw the thief and recognized him, and the thief beat him to death to avoid being caught."

"Blimey," George said, scratching his bald pate. "I never thought of that. I don't know how I'm supposed to take care of all this. I really don't. Sid's no flipping help and—"

" 'Ere, I heard that!"

Sid's shout of outrage made George blink. "All right, all right. Keep your hair on. I only meant they expect too much of us. After all, we're supposed to be retired, not trying to do Scotland Yard's job for them. It's worse than being a London bobby pounding the beat. At least you wouldn't have to work out all these blinking puzzles. The inspector's too busy to bother with the likes of us, and Sid and me have to take care of everything down here. Where's it all going to end, that's what I want to know."

"When the bleeding war's over, that's when." Sid appeared in the doorway. "Beg your pardon, your ladyship."

Elizabeth had sat through George's outburst, nodding sympathetically. Now she rose from her chair, prompting

George to spring to his feet. "Well, I'll let you get on with your lunch." She turned to go, then paused. "Oh, I almost forgot. It seems that Fred Bickham has gone to Ireland to live with his brother. The problem is, he left without paying his rent. I was wondering if you could track him down for me, and get his address. I'd do it myself, but I know how you hate me interfering in police business."

"I don't know as how I can do that, m'm." George looked apologetic. "Ireland's a bit out of my area, so to speak. You'd have to speak to the inspector about that one. Though I don't think Scotland Yard's going to waste their time getting rent money back. Not even for you, your ladyship."

"Probably not." Elizabeth crossed to the door. "But they might if they knew that Fred Bickham might very well have been the last person to see a murdered man alive."

She'd reached the door when George's raised voice stopped her. "Where'd you hear that, then? What's old Fred got to do with Reggie Stewart?"

"I'm not exactly sure," Elizabeth admitted. "But rest assured I'll find out."

George groaned and covered his face with his hands. "I knew it. I blinking knew it."

"Don't worry, George," Elizabeth said cheerfully. "I won't step on anyone's toes."

She left before George could raise any more protests. Not that it would have done any good. She had the bit between her teeth now, so to speak, and she was going to run with it. There were a lot of questions that needed answers, and she was not going to rest until every one of them had been addressed.

Polly stared through the tiny crossed panes of the window, watching the ocean gently lapping at the beach only yards away. Having lunch in a pub was a huge treat for her. Until now, her dining out experience had been limited to

crisps and peanuts at the Tudor Arms, a cup of tea and a
cake at Bessie's, and fish and chips in the High Street,
and that was eaten out of a newspaper while walking
home.

When Sam had suggested they stop at the quaint little
pub for lunch, she'd tried to act as if it were a common
occurrence for her, but seated in a corner window with
her elbows on a white tablecloth, surrounded by polished
brass antiques and pewter tankards, she couldn't seem to
stop squirming in her excitement. This was living. This
was really living. Her fantasy was beginning to come true.

"Penny for them," Sam said, startling her.

"What?"

"Penny for your thoughts. What were you thinking?"

"Oh!" She grinned at him. "I was just thinking how
nice it is to be sitting here with you, having lunch and
all." She picked up her gin and orange and took a sip,
trying not to make a face. She'd ordered her usual drink,
but she wasn't used to drinking gin in the middle of the
day. Somehow it tasted different—sort of bitter. She'd
rather have had a shandy. It wouldn't have made her head
all fuzzy like the gin did. She could just imagine Sam's
face, though, if she'd sat there drinking a mug of beer
watered down with lemonade.

Sam reached out and took hold of her hand. "I thought
you'd enjoy it more than a picnic. Though it was real
sweet of you to bring all that food."

"It wasn't very good food. I'd rather have a plough-
man's lunch any day." She looked down at the slices of
cheese, ham, apple, pickle, and crusty bread that covered
her plate. "I haven't seen this much food on a plate in
years. Wonder how they do it on the ration?"

"I reckon they get special supplies."

"They must do." She took a bite of the tangy Gorgon-
zola cheese and washed it down with the gin.

Sam looked across the room to where a group of young
girls sat laughing together. "I still can't get used to seeing

young kids drinking in the bars. You have to be twenty-one to drink in the States."

"Really?" Polly pulled a face. "Can't see 'em standing for that here. No one takes that much notice of how old you are in the pubs. Unless you're a little kid, of course. Then you'd have to have lemonade."

Sam raised his eyebrows. "They let little kids into the bars?"

"They can go in a pub, but they can't drink beer and stuff. They're supposed to be sixteen, but I've been drinking for two years, and I'm only just sixteen now—" She stopped short, unable to believe she'd actually said the words.

The silence between them seemed to go on and on, while she stared miserably at her plate and prayed that Sam hadn't heard her. Her heart seemed to drop all the way down to her sandals when he said in a strangled voice, "You're *what?*"

For several frantic seconds she considered bluffing her way out, saying she was teasing or something. She'd never been a very good liar, however, and this was one lie she'd been living with for a long time. Too long. It was time she told him. In a way it would be a big relief not to have to pretend anymore.

"Did I hear you right?" Sam shook the hand he was holding. "Polly? You're joking, right? You're twenty-one. Aren't you?"

Slowly she shook her head.

"Just how old are you, then, for chrissake?"

Her lips felt tight and dry and she had to force them to move. "I told you," she whispered. "I'm sixteen."

She didn't dare look at him. He let go of her hand, and a wave of misery swept over her.

"You can't be sixteen . . . you just had a birthday."

"It was my sixteenth birthday."

"You mean . . . you were fifteen until a few weeks ago? All the time we've been seeing each other you were only fifteen?"

His voice sounded weird. She nodded without looking up.

"Jesus Christ." Out of the corner of her eye she saw him lift a half-full glass of ale. Seconds later he put it down empty. "Do you have any idea how much trouble I could be in? Why the hell did you tell me you were twenty when we first met?"

She shrugged. "I thought you wouldn't go out with me if you knew I was only fifteen."

"Damn right I wouldn't."

She tried desperately to think of something to say, anything that would take back the last few minutes and have everything go back to the way it was.

"Finish your lunch," Sam said curtly.

"I'm not hungry." She was never going to eat again. She was afraid she'd lost Sam, and her life would be over. Without him, nothing else mattered. Nothing at all. She just wanted to die.

Elizabeth stood at the door of the bank and glanced up at the huge clock overhead. If she went in now, she'd be late getting back to the Manor House and Violet would never let her hear the last of it. But the opportunity to watch Betty Stewart and Henry Fenworth together was too good to miss. Making up her mind, she stepped inside the quiet building.

She spotted her quarry at once. It wasn't difficult, considering Betty Stewart sat just a few yards away at a desk, across from a dark-haired man who wore black-rimmed spectacles and had a pipe stuck in the corner of his mouth. Apart from an elderly woman at the counter, there were no other customers in the bank.

Elizabeth pretended to be searching in her handbag for something while she strained to hear the conversation going on just out of earshot. The low murmur was too soft to distinguish the words, and she edged closer.

The man's voice was low and soothing; Betty Stewart

seemed agitated. Her voice rose a notch or two, and Elizabeth heard her quite plainly.

"You can believe what you want," she muttered fiercely. "But it's the truth."

Just then, her companion raised his head and caught sight of Elizabeth. He rose to his feet immediately, removing his pipe from his mouth. "Your ladyship! How nice to finally meet you." He edged around the desk and came toward her. "I'm Henry Fenworth, the new manager of this bank. I've seen you in the High Street many times, but I've never had the pleasure of meeting you until now. Your housekeeper, Violet Winters, usually attends to your banking needs, does she not?"

Elizabeth smiled at him. "She did do, Mr. Fenworth, but now that Polly Barnett has taken over as my assistant, she will be taking care of everything in future. I thought I'd come in and inform you of that myself. Just so you know I have authorized her to conduct my business."

It was a brilliant piece of quick thinking, and Elizabeth felt quite pleased with herself. She turned to Betty Stewart, who had risen from her chair and now stood staring at the door as if she were ready to bolt through it at the slightest provocation.

"Good morning, Betty," Elizabeth said, with a friendly nod. "How nice to see you again. I wonder if I might drop by your house later this afternoon. There's something I'd like to discuss with you."

Betty Stewart exchanged a nervous glance with Henry. "If it's about my finances, your ladyship, I'll be able to manage the rent. I'm getting a job at the factory next week, and—"

"No, no, it's not about the rent." Elizabeth glanced at the clock again. "I really don't have time to talk about it now. Perhaps later this afternoon?"

Betty Stewart looked as if she'd like to refuse, but then gave a reluctant nod. "This afternoon, your ladyship."

"Wonderful." Elizabeth beamed at Henry Fenworth,

whose forehead wore deep creases. "So nice to finally meet you, Mr. Fenworth."

"Oh, please, do call me Henry." He hurried to the door and dragged it open for her. "If there's anything I can do for you, please don't hesitate to ask."

Which was awfully decent of him, Elizabeth thought as she hurried outside, considering he had to be well aware of her rocky financial situation. She wondered what he would have said if she'd asked for a large loan. She was almost tempted to find out, but she reminded herself that as lady of the manor, taking out a loan from the bank would be considered quite vulgar.

She arrived back at the manor to find Violet in a nasty temper. Martin was already seated at the kitchen table, though there was no food in front of him. Violet stood over him, berating him for taking the remainder of the rhubarb pie she'd planned on serving for lunch.

She looked up as Elizabeth entered through the back door of the kitchen, while Martin struggled dutifully to his feet.

"Madam! What on earth were you doing out there in the kitchen yard?"

"Digging up vegetables, I shouldn't wonder," Violet snapped, giving her a baleful look. "You're late for lunch, Lizzie. What's left of it after this old fool has scrounged half of it."

"I keep telling you," Martin said, leaning on the table to support his feeble frame, "I haven't taken anything from the larder. It's all I can do to swallow what you put in front of me as it is."

"And what does that mean?" Violet folded her arms and glared at him.

"It means, my dear lady, that your cooking skills are somewhat limited. The results leave much to be desired."

"It's not my cooking that's limited, you old goat, it's the food what's limited. It's not my fault if I can't get butter and cream and eggs. It doesn't help matters when people go creeping around behind my back, stealing whatever they can lay their filthy hands on."

"It's not Martin," Elizabeth said, sinking onto her chair. "It seems there might be a thief sneaking around the village, stealing food and clothes from people's houses."

Martin's bones creaked as he lowered himself carefully onto his chair. "Thank you, madam. I'm glad there's at least one person in this household who doesn't jump to conclusions and make false accusations." He glowered at Violet. "In my day women who spoke out of turn were beaten and thrown in the cellar to consider the error of their ways."

"In your day they were likely chopping the heads off of silly old goats who talked too much," Violet snapped. "Seems like a good idea to me." She turned to Elizabeth. "So what's all this about a thief in the village, then?"

"I heard this morning that another house had been broken into and robbed. It might be an idea to keep that kitchen door locked at night."

"Oh, Lord, whatever next?" Violet placed a plate in front of Elizabeth. "As if we don't have enough to worry about."

"That's pretty much what George said." Elizabeth watched without enthusiasm as Violet ladled minced beef, swimming in gravy, onto her plate.

Violet snorted. "Seems to me them two constables don't have enough to do. What are they doing about finding out who killed Reggie Stewart, then? Nothing, I suppose."

"They're doing their best, I'm sure." Elizabeth picked up her fork and poked at her mashed potatoes. "Tell me, Violet, what do you think of Henry Fenworth?"

"The bank manager?" Violet shrugged her bony shoulders. "He's all right, I s'pose. Bit of a pouf, if you ask me. After all, he's not married and he's got to be at least thirty-five. Ain't natural, that's what I say."

"If you ask me, I'd say the fellow has some jolly good sense," Martin said. "No such thing as a good woman these days. They are entirely too bossy and outspoken."

"Well, nobody asked you, so get on with your lunch before it gets cold."

"How do you know Henry Fenworth isn't married?" Elizabeth gingerly tasted the meat. It wasn't as bad as she'd feared. Violet's skills seemed to be improving lately.

"I know, because I heard some of the women talking about him." Violet brought her plate to the table and sat down. "I think they were trying to get him together with Nellie Smith. She's never been married neither. Make a good pair, them two."

Elizabeth swirled gravy into her mashed potatoes. "Did anyone ever say anything about Betty Stewart and Henry?"

Violet stared at her. "Betty Stewart? She's married, isn't she? Or she was, poor bugger. Besides, she's older than Henry Fenworth. What would she have to do with him, for Gawd's sake?"

That, Elizabeth thought wryly, was a very good question. And one for which she'd dearly love to have an answer.

CHAPTER
❦ 7 ❦

Polly sat in miserable silence as the jeep sped along the country roads. Sam hadn't spoken to her since they'd left Yarmouth. He sat next to her, his face a stone mask. It broke her heart to look at him, so she kept her gaze on the road, not even bothering to remind him when he turned the corners on the wrong side.

Right now she didn't care if she lived or died. All her dreams, her whole future life, had vanished in a second. It was like a bomb had dropped from the sky, and everything that mattered to her had been blown to smithereens.

She knew that Sam had to be really, really angry, because of the way he shot around the bends, almost tipping her out as she rocked from side to side. She should be scared, but somehow she wasn't. It was as if everything inside her had died, and she had no feelings at all. Except for the horrible stabbing pain in her belly. Then again, that could be her drinking gin on an empty stomach.

They screamed around the next bend and took the corner on two wheels. As they rocked upright, Polly's eyes widened. Right in front of them was an old man on a bicycle. It was like he'd appeared out of nowhere. She screeched at the top of her lungs. Sam swore, then everything went crazy. The jeep swerved and bucked across the road, then seemed to sail through the air.

"Hang on!" Sam yelled, but it was too late. Polly felt herself floating free of the jeep, and then everything went black.

"I'm going into the village," Elizabeth said, absently patting Gracie's furry head as the dog rested her jaw on her knee. "I have some errands to run."

"You should let Polly do that for you," Violet said as she immersed a pile of dishes in the soapy suds in the sink. "Where is she, anyway? She didn't come down for her sandwich."

"I gave her the day off." Elizabeth gently pushed the dog away and got to her feet. "I believe she's gone into Yarmouth with her squadron leader."

Violet clicked her tongue. "That child is far too young to be running around with Yanks. Her father wouldn't stand for it if he knew. I can't understand her mother allowing it."

Knowing Polly, Elizabeth doubted that Edna knew about the relationship. She wasn't about to tell Violet that, however. Much as she personally disapproved of Polly's infatuation with the older man, she liked Sam Cutter, and held on to the hope that he would treat Polly with respect.

"I should be back before the applicants get here this afternoon." She paused at the door. "Can I bring something back from the village for supper? We'll have three extra, remember."

"I'll manage." Violet wiped her hands on her apron. I've got some mince left. I'll mix it with some tins of spaghetti and we can have it on toast."

Not exactly a gourmet meal, Elizabeth thought wryly,

but it would have to do. "Well, if I'm not back in time, you get started with the interviews. After all, you're the one who will have the most contact with the new maid. I just hope there will be someone suitable. It's so hard to find anyone willing to do domestic service these days."

"Well, they can't be any worse than Polly," Violet said shortly.

Elizabeth smiled. In spite of Violet's acid comments, she knew quite well that her housekeeper had a soft spot for Polly. If the truth were known, Violet missed having Polly to boss around more than she was willing to admit. The two of them had their spats, but they understood each other. It might not be so easy for Violet to control a London girl. They were far more independent than their country counterparts.

Remembering Polly's comments earlier, she said tentatively, "I think we have to use a little more diplomacy when interviewing these girls. Times have changed, and young women expect more respect from their employers. It's not like it was in my parents' day. Women don't consider themselves servants anymore, and don't want to be treated as such."

Violet sniffed. "All this mollycoddling ... women in trousers, driving buses, building airplanes—where's it going to lead, that's what I want to know. It keeps on like this, we'll have a blinking woman running the country. Then what kind of mess would we all be in, I ask you?"

"Don't worry, Violet. Mr. Churchill would never allow a woman in Downing Street." Elizabeth let the door swing to behind her before Violet could answer.

Still mulling over the problem of finding a decent maid, she almost collided with a tall figure about to descend the stairs to the kitchen.

"Ah, I was hoping I'd find you here." Earl Monroe gave her one of his mesmerizing smiles. "This was my last resort. I've been looking all over the house for you."

Flustered by the warm rush of pleasure at the sight of him, Elizabeth started stuttering. "Oh, M-major! How nice to see you! Is there something I can do for you?"

He took her by the elbow, flustering her even further, and led her into the front hallway. "The officers are giving a cocktail party on the base tomorrow evening," he said, without preamble. "I'd really like it if you would come."

"Oh!" Excitement made her breathless. "Well, how splendid! I'd very much like to come, Major. Thank you."

"Earl," he reminded her. "Remember our pact? There's no one around now to hear you call me by my first name—Elizabeth."

"Oh, right. I'm sorry, Earl. Force of habit, I suppose."

"So, how's the murder investigation going?"

She raised her eyebrows at him. "I really wouldn't know."

He grinned. "Cut the innocent act. You've been running around asking questions all over town."

She tried to look dignified, which was hard, considering that her insides quivered like jelly whenever she looked at him. "And how would you know that? Have you been spying on me?"

"Nope. But your motorbike's been missing for the last couple of days, so I figured you were hot on the track of the murderer."

"I could have been attending to my duties as lady of the manor. I do have responsibilities that have to be taken care of in the village."

"Were you?"

She had to smile. "You'd make a good detective, if you weren't so quick to jump to conclusions."

"Tell you what, you tell me you're not chasing after clues, and I'll surprise you with a gift."

She pursed her lips. "Much as I like gifts, I have to admit to maybe a question or two."

"I thought so." He poked a hand inside his uniform jacket and pulled out a small package. "I brought you a gift, anyway."

For some silly reason, she felt like crying. "For me? How very nice of you, Earl."

He nodded. "It was worth it to hear you call me Earl."

"I would have done that without a gift." She turned it over in her hands. "Thank you."

"You're welcome. I'll pick you up in front of the house tomorrow at six, okay?"

Before she could answer, he'd touched the brim of his cap with his fingers, turned smartly on his heel, and marched down the hall.

She was still unsettled as she approached the front door. So much so that she nearly jumped out of her skin when Martin materialized out of the shadows.

"Allow me, madam." He shuffled over to the door and lifted the heavy iron bar out of its slot.

"How long have you been there, Martin?" Elizabeth asked casually.

"Just a few moments, madam."

"Did you happen to see Major Monroe?"

He blinked at her over the top of his spectacles. Elizabeth often wondered why he bothered to wear them, since he never looked through them. "It is difficult to see anything these days," he said, "with all the blackout curtains shutting out the light."

"The curtains are not drawn yet, Martin."

"You don't say." He looked past her to where light spilled into the hallway from the library. "It's hard to tell. My eyes are not what they used to be."

"Which is why you should be looking through your glasses, not over them." Relieved that her butler had apparently missed her little encounter with the major, Elizabeth stepped through the door. "Martin, we're expecting three young ladies this afternoon. They'll be applying for the job of housemaid. Please show them down to the kitchen when they arrive."

"Yes, Madam. Violet has already advised me of their arrival."

"Thank you, Martin."

"Not at all, madam." Just as the door closed behind her,

she heard him add, "I trust you will enjoy the major's gift, madam."

Ruefully she looked down at the package in her hand. She'd forgotten she was holding it. Tucking it into her pocket, she smiled and ran down the steps.

A few minutes later she arrived at the door of Betty Stewart's house, just in time to see Henry Fenworth coming through the gate.

He gave quite a guilty start when he saw her, and tipped his bowler rather hastily. "Hello again, Lady Elizabeth." He looked back over his shoulder to where Betty Stewart stood at the door. "I . . . er . . . had some business to attend to with Mrs. Stewart. Quite forgot about it this morning. Thought I'd save her the trouble of coming back into town."

"How considerate of you, Mr. Fenworth," Elizabeth said gravely.

"Quite, quite. Well, good day to you, your ladyship." Once more he doffed his bowler, then climbed into a smart little motorcar and roared off up the street.

Betty hovered by the door as Elizabeth walked up the path. "It was so nice of the gentleman to go out of his way," she said, stepping back to allow Elizabeth to enter. "He's really accommodating, for a bank manager."

"So it would seem." Elizabeth stood for a moment in the parlor, adjusting her sight. From some distance away, she heard Caesar bark. He sounded as if he was in the back garden.

"Oh, do please sit down, your ladyship." Betty plumped up a tapestry cushion on the couch. "I've put the kettle on, and I'll make us a nice cup of tea."

"Very good of you," Elizabeth murmured. She waited until Betty had hurried out of the room, then sat down and took a good look around. As before, the place looked clean and tidy. Either the robber had not disturbed very much while he was ransacking the place, or Betty had accomplished a thorough job of tidying up after him.

Everything looked much as it had the last time she was

there. Except the pipe appeared to be missing from its stand on the little table. Elizabeth stared at the wall opposite her. A small rectangle of wallpaper appeared lighter than the rest of the wall, as if something had been covering it. Something that was no longer there.

Elizabeth averted her gaze as Betty returned, carrying a small tray that she set down on the table next to the pipe stand. Handing a steaming cup of tea to Elizabeth, she asked quietly, "One or two?"

"Two, please." Feeling somewhat guilty, Elizabeth watched her spoon sugar into her cup. "Thank you. Most kind, I'm sure." She lifted the cup from its saucer and tasted the tea, then set them down. "Betty, I heard that your house was broken into last night. I wanted to say how sorry I am. On top of everything you've gone through lately, this latest calamity must seem overwhelming."

"It was a shock, yes." Betty sat winding her apron string around her finger. "Thank goodness I wasn't home at the time. I don't know what I would have done if I'd been here all alone."

"Surely your dog would have protected you?"

"Caesar?" Betty uttered a harsh laugh. "Take one step toward that dog, and he's off with his tail between his legs. No flipping watchdog, I can tell you."

"Then it's just as well you weren't here." Elizabeth took a biscuit from the plate Betty offered her. "Thank you." She glanced at the wall. "I hope you didn't lose anything too valuable in the robbery."

"Not really. Mostly clothes and food. Though he did take me mad money out of the dresser drawer, the sod. I was saving up to buy a new dress for the garden fete."

"Oh, I'm sorry." Elizabeth looked at the wall again. "I couldn't help noticing the light patch on the wall."

"Oh, that." Betty stared at it as if seeing it for the first time. "It was a photo of Reggie. Had a thick, solid silver frame. Weighed a ton, it did. The thief must have thought he could hock it at the pawnshop."

"No doubt. I don't suppose you have any idea who the robber might have been? My housekeeper believes that food has been stolen from her larder. It could well have been the same person."

Betty's face registered surprise. "Imagine that. Sorry, your ladyship, I haven't got the slightest idea who would want to steal from me. None at all."

"Well, I suppose we shall have to leave it up to the constables to find out who was responsible."

"It was kind of you to come down, Lady Elizabeth." Betty tugged at the string tangled around her finger.

"Not at all. Tell me, when is the funeral? I'd like to attend."

Betty gave her a strange look. "That's so kind of you. Reggie would have liked that. Not too many people took to my Reggie. He wasn't an easy man to get along with, that's for sure."

"He seemed to get along quite well with Fred Bickham."

Betty's start of surprise was visible. "Fred who?"

"Bickham. He lives—or he did do—at the other end of the village. I believe he's gone to Ireland now to live with his brother. I understand he was quite friendly with your husband, however. They played darts together at the Tudor Arms."

"He never mentioned nothing about him to me. But then again, he was usually drunk by the time he came home from the pub. I never got any sense out of him then."

"So you weren't aware of any real friendship between the two men?"

Betty's laugh was devoid of humor. "I don't think Reggie had a real friend in the entire world. He was a mean man. Mean and nasty."

"Still, it must be hard for you, losing your husband. Sometimes a poor companion can be better than none at all."

"Begging you pardon, m'm, but I have to disagree. This

is the first time I've had any peace in years." Betty drained the last of her tea and set the cup down rather hard. "Besides, I'll be starting work at the factory next week. I'll have plenty of company then."

Nodding, Elizabeth rose. "Well, I wish you luck in your new job." She walked toward the door, then paused, waiting for Betty to open it for her. "By the way, I don't think you told me when the funeral is being held."

"Oh, no, I didn't." Betty's expression was completely without emotion. "It's on Monday. Ten o'clock."

"I'll be there." Elizabeth stepped outside, grateful for the warm sun on her back. "I'll see you at the church, then."

"Yes, your ladyship. Thank you."

"No," Elizabeth said softly. "Thank you."

Betty looked confused for a moment, then closed the door with a decisive thump.

Elizabeth stared at the door for a long moment, then walked slowly down the path and out the gate. From there she could see the back garden of the cottage next door. A line of multicolored washing flapped in the breeze while Joan Plumstone pinned a floral apron to the line.

Elizabeth hesitated for a moment, then made up her mind. A few seconds later she rounded the wall of the cottage and came upon Joan still pegging up the damp clothes. The woman spun around at the sound of her voice.

"Lady Elizabeth! You quite startled me. I didn't hear you coming."

"I do apologize." Elizabeth nodded at the washing. "I can see you're busy. Perhaps this isn't a good time."

"I always have time for visitors such as yourself." Joan picked up the empty washing basket. "Can I offer you a cup of tea?"

"Oh, no, thank you. I won't be more than a moment or two." Elizabeth gestured at Betty Stewart's cottage. "I've just been talking to your neighbor. She tells me her house was broken into last night."

Joan tutted. "Don't know what the world's coming to, I don't. The war is making villains of us all, I swear. Makes you afraid to step outside your door, it does."

"Yes, well, at least he doesn't seem to be a violent man. Just hungry, by the sound of it. He took mostly food and clothes."

"So I heard." Joan carried the basket to her back door. "Still, it's frightening to think someone can just walk into your house and take what he wants."

Elizabeth followed her. "Betty said he took a photograph of her husband from the wall. How sad, considering the poor man has just died."

"Oh, I don't think Betty's too broken up by it, if you ask me." Joan sent a furtive glance at the neighboring cottage. "They were never happy, you know. Slept in separate bedrooms. Betty wouldn't have him in her bed. She told me she couldn't stand him near her, 'cause of the coal dust. Said he was always filthy. I bet she's glad that thief took that picture. She always hated it. It was taken when Reggie won the hundred-yard dash at the North Horsham races. Proud as a peacock of that, he was. Always bragging about it. Drove Betty crazy, it did. She said that photo was the only thing he cared about in the whole world."

"Really," Elizabeth murmured. "How interesting." She realized Joan was staring at her, and added hastily, "Well, I really must run along. I just wanted to make sure you knew about the robbery and to warn you to lock your doors at night. We can't be too careful nowadays."

"Don't I know it." Joan heaved the empty basket higher on her hip. "Thank you for stopping by, your ladyship."

"Not at all." Conscious of the time fleeting by, Elizabeth hurried back to her motorbike. The applicants for the position of housemaid would be arriving any minute.

As she sailed up the hill toward the manor, she turned over in her mind Joan's comments about the photograph that had been stolen. Or perhaps it hadn't been stolen at all.

So far, the murder weapon had not been found. Was it possible that a simple framed photograph could have done that much damage to Reggie's face?

She rather doubted it. It could, however, have started a fight that became ugly, perhaps getting broken in the process and causing tempers to escalate. The question was, if Reggie did die of a heart attack caused by the beating, would it still be a case of murder? If not, it might be possible to get a confession, once she was sure of the identity of the person responsible.

Right now, all she had were hunches and supposition. As she had learned through experience, that was not nearly enough to consider a person suspect. She needed proof. Finding the murder weapon would help considerably.

Her thoughts came to an abrupt halt as she spied three young women trudging up the hill ahead of her. Apparently her applicants had arrived. She squeezed her horn and roared past them without acknowledging them. First impressions were important, and she had no wish to present herself to a future servant . . . no, employee, as a speed maniac on a motorcycle with goggles awry and her best straw hat strung around her neck on flimsy elastic and flapping wildly behind her. That wouldn't do at all.

CHAPTER

🙰 8 🙰

"You must be Sadie Buttons." Elizabeth picked up the sheet of paper lying in front of her and studied it. "I see you've been in domestic service in London."

"Yes, m'm. Three years, or thereabouts."

"Your references seem satisfactory." Elizabeth laid down the paper and gazed at the young woman seated on the other side of her office desk. "Tell me, why do you want to live in Sitting Marsh?"

Sadie's pert features screwed up into a grimace. Her curly dark brown hair had been parted and secured into bunches with rubber bands. They stuck out on each side of her face, which had been scrubbed clean of makeup, making her look younger than her eighteen years.

She sat twisting her hands in her lap, as if afraid they might get away from her. "I'll go any place what doesn't have bombs dropping on it. Been bombed out twice, I have. Last time I was buried for three hours before they dug us out. I was in the lav at the time. Only room left standing by the time it was all over. I couldn't get out, though, 'cause of the rubble blocking the door."

"Oh, my goodness." Elizabeth stared at her in horror. "How absolutely awful for you."

"Yes, m'm. It were."

"What about your family? Where are they?"

Sadie shrugged. "Me dad and me bruvver's in the Army. Me mum's got a new boyfriend. She's never home. She won't even know I'm gone."

"But you do intend to let her know where you are, should you get the position?"

Sadie looked at her with solemn gray eyes. "What for?"

Elizabeth felt a strong pang of sympathy for the young girl. It sounded as though her home life left a lot to be desired. "Well, as you know, a housemaid's work can be quite strenuous. Especially in a house this size. Unfortunately, we can't offer you a great deal of help. Violet, the housekeeper, does her best, but the brunt of the work would fall on you."

Sadie looked doubtful. "It's an awfully big house."

"Yes, well, I don't expect you to keep it all clean, of course. Most of it is shut off, and Violet takes care of the kitchen, as well as the butler's room and her private quarters. Your duties would be mostly my bedroom and office, the bathrooms, the library and conservatory, the drawing room and dining room. Then there's the east wing. Normally that would be closed off, but now that the American officers are billeted there, I'm afraid it will have to be included. I'm told, however, that the officers take excellent care of their quarters, so that shouldn't be much of a problem."

Sadie nodded. "I reckon I can handle that all right."

Elizabeth eyed her stocky figure. She had good shoulders on her, and thick arms. She appeared to be a lot more robust than Polly, whose slender frame nevertheless had a surprising amount of strength and stamina. "You'd have to find somewhere to live in the village, of course. But that could be arranged. As a matter of fact, I have a cottage to rent—"

"I was hoping I could live here, your ladyship."

Taken aback, Elizabeth said quickly, "Oh, I really don't think—"

"Lady Elizabeth"—Sadie leaned forward, her eyes wide in her earnest face—"I'm a good worker, I am. My last employer would tell you that—if she was still alive. Me mum don't want me, me friends have all moved out of the smoke, and I hate living by meself. Gives me the willies, it does, ever since I got bombed out. I don't need no fancy room. I'd sleep in the stables if you like. If you let me live here, I'll work me fingers to the bone for you, I swear, honest to God. I'll have this whole place gleaming like gold, you just see."

Elizabeth leaned back in her chair. There was no doubt about the girl's enthusiasm. "I hadn't really planned on hiring a live-in," she said cautiously. "I'll have to think about it. In any case, I haven't yet made up my mind who will be hired for the position. Since all three of you will be staying here for the night, Violet will be talking to all of you over supper. She and I will discuss the matter later, and we'll make the decision in the morning."

"Yes, m'm." Sadie got slowly to her feet. "I can't tell you how bad I want this job, your ladyship. It means a lot to me."

Her desperation concerned Elizabeth a great deal. "I can see that. I'll let you know what we decide in the morning."

"Yes, m'm. Thank you, m'm." The girl looked most unhappy as she moved to the door. Obviously she didn't have much confidence in her chances of being employed.

Much as she needed a housemaid, Elizabeth reminded herself, she couldn't allow her sympathy to cloud her judgment. There was also the matter of Violet's opinion. Her housekeeper would not be swayed by emotions. During the following two interviews, however, she had trouble keeping Sadie's fervent face out of her mind.

As the third applicant left the office, Elizabeth found herself hoping that Violet would want to hire Sadie Buttons. Though all three girls were qualified for the position, only Sadie had made it sound as if she'd break her back for the chance of being employed at the Manor House. Though how Violet would accept the idea of the girl living in the mansion was another question entirely.

Since the girls would be taking their evening meal in the kitchen, Elizabeth had elected to have a light meal alone in the conservatory. Though this was her favorite room in which to relax, she rarely dined there, preferring to take her meals with Violet and Martin in the huge, warm kitchen where she had spent so many happy hours of her childhood.

She'd escaped to the kitchen every chance she had, despite her mother's objections and her father's outright disapproval. As an only child, she'd spent too many lonely hours in her bedroom, or the schoolroom with her tutor. She'd adored the hustle and bustle of the busy kitchen, with its jovial staff of maids and cooks, and the occasional visits of a stable lad or two. The contrast between her parents' somber lifestyle and the cheerful hubbub of the kitchen was like night and day.

Now the conservatory served as her private refuge. A quiet, peaceful room that in the daytime allowed a view of the rolling lawn and gardens through its floor-to-ceiling windows. At night the view was obscured by the despised blackout curtains, though the room managed to retain the cozy feeling of being secluded from the rest of the house. Here Elizabeth could relax and forget the torments of her busy life.

Violet rarely disturbed her in this tranquil sanctuary, unless it was an emergency. She was therefore surprised to hear a tap on the door and see the head of her housekeeper peeking around it. "Major Monroe to see you," she muttered. "I suppose you want me to show him in."

Aware of Violet's disapproval of her friendship with the major, Elizabeth merely smiled. "If you would, Violet.

Thank you. And I'm finished with my tray, if you'd like to take it with you."

She could tell Violet was holding her tongue with the greatest of difficulty as she took the tray and left the room. A moment or two later another tap accelerated Elizabeth's heartbeat.

"Come in!" she sang out, and hastily brushed crumbs from her skirt before gazing expectantly at the opening door.

The moment he came into the room, she knew something was wrong. His ruggedly handsome face, usually wreathed in smiles when he greeted her, seemed strained and tired. His eyes were bleak, and he avoided looking at her directly, as if wary of giving his thoughts away.

She leaned forward, heart racing with apprehension. "What is it? What's wrong?"

He sat down heavily, and reached for her hand.

With mixed emotions, she waited for him to speak.

It was some time before he did so. When he finally spoke, his words struck a chill in her heart. "Elizabeth, something's happened, and I can't think of any way to make it easy for you."

"You've been called back to America." It was the thing she'd dreaded ever since she'd first realized how she felt about him.

For the first time he met her gaze, and something in his eyes made her pulse leap. "No, that's not it."

Relief made her heady. "Then whatever it is, I'm sure it can't be as bad as you think."

He turned her hand palm up in his own warm hands. "Elizabeth, there's been an accident. A bad one. Squadron Leader Sam Cutter's in the hospital in North Horsham. He's in a coma, and the medics don't know if he's going to make it."

Elizabeth wrinkled her brow. "Sam Cutter? But I thought he was on leave. He was supposed to go to Yarmouth today with Polly. . . ." Her voice trailed off when she saw Earl's expression. "Oh, no. Please, not Polly."

"She's in the hospital, too," Earl said quickly. "That's all I know. They won't tell me any more than that. I thought maybe you would want—"

He broke off as Elizabeth rose abruptly to her feet. "I'd like to see her."

"I thought you might. I'll take you."

She struggled to keep her thoughts coherent. "What about her mother? Does she know?"

"She went with her to the hospital. I believe her sister went, too."

She realized, then, that he was still holding her hand. How she longed to feel his arms holding her close. Arms to which she had no right. "I must tell Violet, and get my coat. The sea breeze is so cool at night—" Her voice wavered, and she swallowed hard.

He let go of her hand and held her gently by her upper arms. "Elizabeth, it might not be protocol or whatever, but it's okay by me if you want to let it all out. I have a big shoulder you can cry on."

She would never know how she held on to her composure in that moment. Maybe it was her upbringing that gave her the strength. Or maybe it was the fear that if she once "let it all out" as he suggested, she might very well lose her reserve altogether and reveal her feelings for him—which, she was quite sure, would be a disastrous mistake.

Instead she raised her chin. "Thank you, Earl. I truly appreciate your concern. I'm extremely grateful for your offer of a lift to the hospital, and if you'll give me a few minutes, I'll meet you at the front door."

His expression was rueful as he let her go. "The British stiff upper lip wins the day. One of these days, Lady Elizabeth, you're going to lose that iron control of yours. I kind of hope I'm there to see it." He left rather abruptly, while she wallowed in confusion, wondering exactly what he meant and if she'd offended him in some way.

She had little time to ponder on it, however. She hurried down to the kitchen and quickly told Violet the dreadful news.

"Poor little mite." Violet stacked a wet plate on the draining board. "What a nasty shock for her mother. I do hope she's going to be all right. Do you want me to come with you to the hospital?"

"No, no, you need to stay here and take care of our guests."

"Not exactly guests, are they?" Violet squinted at her. "You going to be all right, Lizzie? Try not to worry. Polly's a lot stronger than she looks."

"I know it's silly," Elizabeth admitted, "but I think of Polly as family. She's like a daughter—or a younger sister—oh, I don't know. I just know that if . . . something . . . should happen to her, it would break my heart."

"I know. I'm fond of her, too." Violet wiped her hands on her apron. "But let's not get all worked up over what might be nothing. Polly's young, and she's a fighter. She'll pull through. You'll see."

Elizabeth grabbed Violet's hands. "Violet, I pray that you're right. Now I must run. Earl is taking me to the hospital."

For once Violet raised no objections. "Give her my love." She tried to smile, but it worried Elizabeth to see the fear in her eyes. "Tell her she'll do anything to get out of working."

Elizabeth fled from the kitchen before her resolve cracked and she bawled like a baby.

Earl stood waiting for her in the hallway when she came down from her bedroom a few minutes later. If he'd been miffed at her earlier, he gave no sign of it as they sped along the dark, windswept road to North Horsham.

"You didn't tell me what happened," she said, more to break the awkward silence than out of any desire to hear the details. "What kind of accident was it?"

"I don't know much. The MP told me Sam was driving too fast and swerved to miss a guy on a bike. The jeep overturned. Polly was thrown clear, but Sam was trapped underneath. The jeep dragged him down the road. His face is pretty badly scraped, and he broke his arm and a couple of ribs."

"Poor Sam. To have survived all that danger in the skies, only to meet it on the ground." She inhaled, breathing in the salty air. Somehow the beach smelled different at night—the aroma of seaweed and wet sand was made more pronounced by the night breezes. It reminded her of the old days, before the world had gone crazy. She swallowed around a lump in her throat. "They didn't tell you anything at all about Polly?"

"Only that she'd been taken to the hospital. Sorry, Elizabeth. I'd tell you if I knew more."

"That's all right. I suppose I could have rung the hospital. Then again, they might not have told me anything either. At least if I'm there, I can insist on talking to someone about Polly."

"That's my girl."

Momentarily distracted by the thought of being referred to as Earl's "girl," Elizabeth was unprepared when he added, "So what did you think of my gift?"

She caught her breath, unwilling to admit she'd actually forgotten about it. "I'm sorry, Earl, really I am. I haven't opened it yet. Things have been rather hectic lately, and I've been so preoccupied. . . ."

"That's okay. I know I'm way down on your list of priorities."

Realizing he was hurt, she felt like sobbing. How could she possibly have forgotten a gift from him? She patted the pocket of her coat, satisfying herself that the slight bulge was still there. "I wanted to wait until I had time to myself to enjoy opening it," she offered, hoping he'd accept her excuse.

She couldn't see his face clearly in the dark, but she could hear the restraint in his voice when he answered. "It's no big deal. You've got a lot on your mind lately. How's the murder investigation coming along? Have the cops found out who killed the guy yet?"

"I don't think they have the slightest idea."

He must have read something in her voice, for he sounded intrigued when he asked, "But *you* do?"

She smiled in the darkness. "I have a theory, yes, but I don't know how well it holds up. It's mostly conjecture, I'm afraid. That can be dangerous when dealing with a murder case."

"Anything is dangerous when you're dealing with murder. I figured you'd know that by now."

"I do." She was silent for a moment, then added, "The constables are not doing their job the way they should. I think they both are so resentful at having to come out of retirement that they do as little as possible. I sometimes wonder if they believe that if they don't do their job, they'll be released from their duties and can go back to their easy life."

"Could be. Would that happen?"

Elizabeth sighed. "Unfortunately for them, I'm afraid not. George and Sid are stuck with the job until the war is over. With most of our men serving in the forces, that doesn't leave much in the way of efficient professionals to run the towns and villages. We have to take what we can get. Nowadays the women are taking over most of the responsible positions, and doing very well. One can't help wondering how well they will adapt when the war is over and they have to go back to being housewives again."

"Does make you wonder. In the meantime, you're trying to do the constables' job as well as your own."

"Not very well, I'm afraid."

"Oh, I wouldn't say that. I seem to remember your solving a sticky case or two in the past."

"Well, I don't think I'm going to solve this one. There doesn't seem to be any way to get the proof I need to support my theory."

"You haven't told me what your theory is yet."

She glanced at him, wishing she could see his face. He was very good at hiding his feelings under that well-modulated drawl, but sometimes she could tell his mood by his eyes. She had the feeling that he was unhappy with her, though she wasn't quite sure why. "I haven't, have I?"

"None of my business?"

"No, of course it's not that. It's just that I hesitate to point an accusing finger at someone with no justification other than a vague hunch."

"Hey, it's only me. I'm not going to blab it all over town."

Anxious to dispel the feeling of having upset him, she quickly capitulated. "Well, do you remember when we visited Betty Stewart to tell her that her husband had been found murdered?"

"I remember."

"I noticed that the door to the kitchen was open, yet her dog didn't bother to come into the parlor, in spite of people being in there."

"He could have been tied up."

"True, but I remembered later that Betty had told us she'd shut him up in a room. I don't think it was the dog making that noise in the kitchen."

"Then who was it?"

"Well, I noticed a pipe on the table next to the couch."

"Her husband's?"

"I don't think so. When I touched it, it was warm, as if someone had recently smoked it. I doubt if Betty smokes a pipe. I'm sure Joan Plumstone would have told me if she does. Joan was remarkably full of information when I talked to her."

"So who did the pipe belong to?"

"I think it belonged to the bank manager. What's more, I think he was there in the Stewart house that night. Joan told me that she overheard Betty in a terrible argument with her husband about her interest in Henry Fenworth."

"They had something going on?"

"It's entirely possible. I think Reggie Stewart might have come home earlier than expected and found his wife

with Henry Fenworth. If so, he and Henry could have
fought. According to the doctor, Reggie died from a heart
attack that was probably brought on by the beating. Perhaps Henry thought he'd killed him, and panicked. Or
perhaps Betty Stewart killed her husband in self-defense
later. There's no way of knowing what happened without
some kind of proof."

"That's quite a theory.

"I know. It's all guesswork, of course. When I went
back to the house later, I noticed a space on the wall
where a picture had been. Betty Stewart said it had been
stolen, along with some other things from her house. She
said it was in a heavy silver frame."

There was a short pause before he said slowly, "I'm
not sure I'm following you."

"Well, there was also a pair of candlesticks on the mantelpiece. Antique silver, I should imagine, and quite valuable. I had to wonder why the thief didn't take them as
well, if he went to the trouble of removing a photograph
from the wall for the frame."

"So you think . . . ?"

"I think that Henry could have snatched the frame from
the wall to use as a weapon, no doubt to defend himself,
since Reggie Stewart was a great deal heavier, and probably stronger."

Earl didn't answer for a long moment. "Heavy candlesticks?"

"Very heavy, I should imagine."

"Wouldn't a heavy candlestick make a better weapon?
Easier to grab hold of in the heat of the moment, I'd say."

"If he was close enough to reach them."

"True. So you need to find the photo frame, is that it?"

"I need to find the murder weapon, whatever it is."
Elizabeth sighed. "George is supposed to be looking for
it, but to tell you the truth, I don't think he's too enthu-
siastic. Ever since he found out that Reggie Stewart died
from a heart attack, he's treating it as natural causes."

"That's crazy. Someone beat the poor guy beyond recognition and buried him with a bunch of potatoes. That's not natural causes."

"I know. Once the inspector hears word of it, I'm sure he'll want a proper investigation. George just isn't in any hurry to let him know about it." She sat up straighter as they crested the brow of a hill and she could see the lights of North Horsham below. "We're nearly there." She felt cold, and wrapped her arms around herself for comfort. "Oh, Earl, pray that Polly is all right. It's my fault she went to Yarmouth. I knew her mother wouldn't approve, yet I said nothing to stop her."

"Would she have listened to you if you had?"

"Probably not." Elizabeth stared miserably at the lights growing brighter by the second. "I just know that if she's badly hurt, or . . . worse, I'll never be able to forgive myself."

CHAPTER
❀ 9 ❀

The glare of lights inside the hospital foyer hurt Elizabeth's eyes as she hurried with Earl to the admittance desk. At first the young nurse on duty was reluctant to tell them where to find Polly, but upon learning Elizabeth's identity, she became far more accommodating.

"Polly's been worried about her job, your ladyship," the nurse explained, after giving Elizabeth the number of her room. "She was going on and on about it. I think it means a lot to her."

"How is she?" Elizabeth asked anxiously. "Is she badly hurt?"

"She'll be right as rain in a few days." The nurse gave Earl a dazzling smile and fluttered her eyelashes. "Just a few bumps and scrapes. A load of hay broke her fall. She sailed right over a hedge. Lucky for her that haystack was there."

Elizabeth let out her breath in a rush of relief. "Can we see her now?"

"Of course." The nurse simpered at Earl with a disgusting lack of decorum. "Anything for our handsome boys in blue, that's what I say!"

"Well, how fortunate that I thought to bring him along," Elizabeth muttered.

Earl seemed not to notice the nurse's interest. "Can you tell me how Squadron Leader Sam Cutter is doing? He was brought in with Polly."

The nurse's frown of concern was not encouraging. "Oh, that one wasn't so lucky. He got dragged underneath the jeep. Made a mess of his face. He'll end up with a few scars over this one, I'm afraid."

"But he *is* going to recover?"

She looked wary. "I really can't say. He's unconscious right now. You'd have to ask the doctor about that."

"I'd like to see him," Earl said firmly.

The nurse hesitated, then gave him a quick nod. "I'll talk to the doctor. Come back here after you've visited Polly Barnett, and I'll let you know then if you can see the squadron leader."

"Perhaps he could see Sam Cutter while I'm visiting Polly," Elizabeth suggested.

"I'll see what I can do, your ladyship."

The nurse hurried off, and Elizabeth smiled up at Earl. "I'll meet you back here later. I hope things go well for him."

"So do I. Thanks, Elizabeth."

Her heart too full for words, she nodded, then hurried down the corridor to Polly's room.

Edna and Marlene sat on either side of Polly's bed, and both jumped to their feet when Elizabeth opened the door.

"Lady Elizabeth! How kind of you to come," Edna said. Her eyes were red-rimmed, as if she'd been crying, and Marlene's face was white with shock.

As for Polly, she looked the best of the three, though

a white bandage covered her forehead and another encased her right elbow. "I'm so sorry, m'm," she cried, when she saw Elizabeth in the doorway. "I really am. I'll be back at work tomorrow, I promise. I know we've got a lot to do, what with the maids being down here for interviews and all. The doctor says I can leave in the morning."

Elizabeth caught the look of alarm on Edna's face and moved into the room. "Nonsense, Polly, you must stay at home until you are perfectly well. Don't worry about the work. We can catch up when you come back."

Polly seemed unconvinced. "I don't want no one else doing my work, m'm."

So that's what had been worrying the child. Elizabeth smiled. "Polly, the three applicants from London are maids. They're not after your job."

"I was a maid, too, your ladyship, before I got to be your assistant."

"And you will continue to be my assistant, so stop worrying." She gave Edna an encouraging nod. "I'm happy to see your daughter looking so well. She gave us all quite a fright."

"She did, indeed, your ladyship." Edna frowned at Polly. "I still want to know what she was doing riding in a jeep with an American airman this afternoon, when she was supposed to be at work in the manor."

"I'm sorry, Mrs. Barnett," Elizabeth said smoothly. "I gave her permission to go. I bitterly regret that it ended this way." Normally, she wouldn't have considered intruding to save her young assistant, but right now wasn't the time for Polly to be forced to answer a lot of awkward questions, especially with Sam Cutter lying in a coma.

The look of pure gratitude in Polly's eyes was mirrored in those of her sister, who spoke for the first time. "That's really kind of you, Lady Elizabeth."

Making up her mind to have a stern word with Polly once all this was over, Elizabeth said briskly, "Well, I have to get back to the Manor House. Please take care of yourself, Polly, and don't be in too much of a hurry to come back to work. We can manage without you for a few days."

"Thank you, m'm. I don't suppose you've heard how Sam Cutter is doing?"

The fear on Polly's face made Elizabeth ache for her. "I haven't, I'm afraid. Major Monroe is waiting for permission to see him now. If there is any news, I'll ask the nurse to let you know."

"Thank you, m'm. I really would appreciate it."

Elizabeth left the room, wishing she could be more positive about Sam Cutter's condition. The fact that Earl was so worried about him didn't bode well for the young man. She walked back to the foyer, praying that he would make it through.

Earl was not in the foyer when she returned, and she joined the rest of the people waiting patiently on the long, hard seats. Several minutes passed before she spied him striding down the corridor toward her. One look at his face told her the news wasn't good.

She rose and hurried toward him, wishing with all her heart she could give him a warm hug. "How is he?" The question was mechanical. She already knew the answer.

"No change." He looked tired, his mouth drooping at the corners. "Even if he makes it, I doubt anyone's going to recognize him for a while."

"That bad?" He started down the corridor, and she hurried to keep up with him.

"From what they tell me. His face is covered in bandages, so it's hard for me to see for myself."

"Will you have to tell his family?"

"They already know. They can't get here to see him. All they can do is wait. I didn't know what to say to them. What the hell could I say to them?"

She couldn't bear to see him like this. Abandoning protocol, she reached for his hand and gave it a firm squeeze. "You can't wrap your men up in a cocoon and protect them from harm, Earl. What happened isn't your fault."

"Then why do I feel it is? And why is it Sam who always seems to end up in trouble? He's a decent guy, and one of the bravest men I've known. He doesn't deserve this."

They passed through the door, and he let it swing to behind them, shutting them out from the light. For several paces he didn't say anything, then the words burst out. "Dammit, Elizabeth, he was on the ground. If he'd been shot down, or had to bail out, it would at least have been while he was doing what he'd come over here to do. But a goddamn car wreck? The whole thing is such a hell of a waste."

She pulled up and stepped in front of him. She couldn't see his expression in the dark. She could only guess, by the torment in his voice, how awful he felt. "Listen to me. Sam's a strong, healthy young man. He'll pull through this. You'll see. He'll be back in the skies before you know it. Doing what he came over here to do."

"I hope you're right, Elizabeth. I hope to God you're right. It's tough enough to deal with it when a good man doesn't come back from a mission. But to lose him this way . . . it's so damn senseless."

Words poured into her mind, but none of them made any sense at all. There had to be some encouraging, reassuring words she could say to him. If there were, she couldn't think of them. "We had better be getting back to the manor," she said at last. It seemed the safest thing to say at that point.

Somehow they found the jeep in the darkened car park, and when Earl fired the engine, the roar was deafening. Thankful for the wind that cooled her burning face, Elizabeth thought miserably of all the things she'd wanted to say. Anything to let him know that she understood, and longed to comfort him. Dangerous words that might well have led to exposing her heartheld secret.

But it was too late now. It had always been too late, from the moment she'd discovered he was married. Perhaps it was just as well. Nevertheless, she would always carry an ache in her heart for what might have been.

Elizabeth awoke the next morning with a melancholy that seemed to follow her like a fog. Earl had seemed subdued when he'd said good night, and she had lain awake for hours before drifting into an uneasy sleep.

Somehow she managed to get through breakfast without Violet's sharp gaze perceiving her sour mood, and was cheered somewhat by her housekeeper's announcement that Sadie Buttons was her choice for the new maid. "The girl's got a mind like a steel trap," she said, with a light in her eyes that suggested she was ready for a challenge. "That could become a problem if I let it, but she's got stamina and a strong back, and seems really anxious to do the job. She's more than willing to do anything I ask. At least for now. I think she'll fit in very nicely down here. She's not like the rest of them, wishy-washy, wanting to know how much time they got off and turning their noses up when I mention cleaning the lavatories."

"I heartily agree with your decision. I'll leave it up to you to let the other two know our decision."

"I already have. They've had breakfast and are on their way back to London."

"Of course. I forgot how early the bus leaves." Elizabeth hesitated, then added, "Did Sadie happen to mention that she wanted to live here at the manor?"

"She did. I told her it would be up to you, of course, but if you ask me, I think it will be a good thing. She'd be instantly available that way, wouldn't she? After all, maids always used to live here in the old days."

"I agree. When will she be moving down here?"

"In the next day or two. Her room is all ready for her. Just as well, with Polly laid up. Did she say how long before she can come back to work?"

"A few days. She seemed anxious to come back to work."

"Didn't want you to notice how much she gets away

with in the office, I don't doubt," Violet said tartly, though Elizabeth could tell she was hugely relieved to hear that Polly wasn't badly hurt. "Anyway, we'll have a new maid now."

"Then that's settled," Elizabeth said, immensely relieved that at least one problem had been solved with reasonable ease. Even so, she couldn't shake the lethargy that plagued her.

Even the antics of George and Gracie failed to cheer her that morning as she romped with them on the lawn, and she returned to the house determined to dispel the uneasiness that would not let her relax.

She could not allow herself to mope around the office, however. Vowing to plunge herself into something that would take her mind off her personal problems, she concentrated on the thorny issue of Reggie Stewart's murder.

Somewhere in the back of her mind a question niggled, but she couldn't seem to pin it down. She needed to ask more questions, dig a little deeper. With that in mind, she rode her motorcycle down to the village and wound her way along the coast road to the Tudor Arms.

Alfie, the bartender, was setting up for the lunchtime trade when she arrived, and seemed surprised to see her. "Lady Elizabeth! This is a pleasant surprise!" He set a small glass of cream sherry on the counter. "Don't tell no one," he said with a sly wink. "There's still five minutes to go before opening time."

Elizabeth gazed longingly at the glass. "Well, it is a little early to be drinking sherry."

"Go on, your ladyship, live a little dangerously. It's wartime, after all, ain't it? Who knows how long we've got on this earth? Live for the moment, that's what I say. Tomorrow might never come."

"Well, it wouldn't do for all of us to think that way." The inviting fragrance of the sherry wafted by her nose. "Oh, well, why not?" She reached for the glass and lifted it to her lips.

"That's the spirit, m'm. A little bit of what you fancy does you good, I always say."

"Do you indeed?" Elizabeth murmured.

Alfie swiped at the counter with a damp cloth. "Anyway, what can I do you for?"

Elizabeth raised her eyebrows.

"Sorry, m'm, it's a phrase they keep using on *ITMA*— that new radio show. Stands for It's That Man Again."

"So I heard. It appears to be very popular."

"Oh, it is, m'm, I can tell you. It's good to get a laugh now and then on the radio. The news is always bad these days. I get so I'm afraid to turn it on sometimes."

"Yes, well, we do need to keep informed, Alfie. It wouldn't do to bury our heads in the sand and pretend there's no war going on."

"Bit hard to do that nowadays, what with all our blokes fighting overseas, and the pub full of foreigners. Can't understand half of what these Yanks say. Thought they was supposed to be talking English."

"We are probably just as difficult for them to understand." Elizabeth glanced at the clock on the wall above Alfie's head. "Is that the time? I must be off. There is one thing, though, I want to ask you before I go, Alfie."

"Thought so, m'm. You don't usually come in here unless you have something on your mind."

"I was just wondering if you remember seeing Reggie Stewart in here about a week ago. Captain Carbunkle said he saw him playing darts in the public bar."

Alfie wrinkled his face in thought. "Yeah, now I come to think of it, he *was* in here. Playing with old Fred Bickham, he was."

"Was it a friendly game?"

Alfie's gaze sharpened. "Friendly? I reckon it was. They left together, and they seemed like they was getting along all right. Tell you the truth, I was a bit surprised. Not many people got along with Reggie. Had a nasty temper, that one. And Fred, well, he's a bit of a loner. He usually don't mix with the other blokes. I think that's the first time I ever saw him playing darts."

"Perhaps he was celebrating."

Alfie's eyes widened. "Celebrating? If he was, he didn't say nothing. Why, was it his birthday or something?"

Elizabeth sipped her sherry before answering. "I understand that Fred Bickham has moved to Ireland. He intends to live with his brother."

Alfie's surprise turned to amazement. "Go on! We talking about the same Fred? Far as I knew he didn't have no brother. He told me the only family he had left was a sister living in Devon, and she didn't talk to him no more."

Elizabeth set her glass carefully on the counter. "Really? Then I must be mistaken. Perhaps it was his birthday, after all."

"I tell you one thing," Alfie said, "they was both knocking them back that night. Weren't too steady, neither of them, by the time they left."

"Do you happen to know what time that was, thereabouts?"

Alfie grinned. "I can tell you the exact time, your ladyship. It was ten minutes to eleven by my clock." He jerked a thumb at the clock behind him. "See, Reggie asked me what time it was, just as they was leaving. Fred laughed at him. Said my clock was running five minutes fast. I told him it was his watch what was slow, but he said all the pubs run their clocks five minutes fast to get the customers out on time."

Elizabeth glanced at the clock. "Was he right?"

"Ah, that'd be telling, wouldn't it, m'm?"

"I suppose it would. Did you happen to see either Fred or Reggie after that night?"

Alfie tilted his head to one side. "Now that you mention it, m'm, I can't say as I've seen either one of them. They haven't been in here, that's for sure."

Elizabeth slid off her seat. "Well, I must be off. Thank you for the sherry, Alfie."

"Pleasure, m'm. Happy to serve you anytime." She was almost at the door when he added, "By the way, m'm, do the constables know who buried poor old Reggie in the garden?"

"Not yet, as far as I know."

"Strange business, that." Alfie shook his head. "I mean, if the guy died of a heart attack, why would someone bury him?"

"Probably because whoever had beaten him thought he'd killed him."

"Ah, that makes sense. Sort of panicked, I suppose."

Elizabeth sighed. "Something like that."

"Here, you don' think it was Fred, do you? He don't look strong enough to beat up a bloke like Reggie. Why, Reggie would have killed him with one hand tied behind his back. I'd lay odds on that."

"I have to admit," Elizabeth said, as she went out the door, "that same thought had occurred to me."

Henry Fenworth looked up when Elizabeth approached his desk, and smiled rather nervously as he rose to his feet. "Lady Elizabeth, how lovely to see you. To what do I owe this very distinct pleasure?"

Elizabeth sank onto the comfortable chair opposite him and waited for him to do likewise. When he was settled, she lowered her voice and said softly, "I have a rather delicate matter to discuss with you, Mr. Fenworth."

"Henry, please, your ladyship. There's no need to be so formal here at Westminster Bank." Henry pulled off his glasses and withdrew a large, white handkerchief from his top pocket. "I understand the nature of your concerns." With great vigor he began polishing his glasses with the handkerchief. "If you are here to ask for a loan, we shall have to consider very carefully—"

"Mr. Fenworth . . . Henry." Elizabeth leaned forward. "I'm afraid what I have to ask is of a more personal nature."

Henry stopped polishing. "Oh, really?"

"I have to ask you where you were and what you were doing a week ago last Saturday."

Henry's thin eyebrows twitched. He replaced his glasses and looked rather coldly at her. "May I respectfully ask, Lady Elizabeth, exactly what business it is of yours?"

Elizabeth smiled. "Well, of course, if you'd rather talk to the constables, I'm sure that can be arranged."

Henry narrowed his eyes. "I don't think that will be necessary. I have nothing to hide. A week ago last Saturday I was here at the bank until noon. When I left here, I drove immediately to North Horsham, where I met with a client. I dined at his home and left there shortly after midnight."

"And your client could verify that if asked?"

"Of course." Although Henry's frown appeared genuine, Elizabeth detected a certain wariness in his eyes. "May I ask why you want to know?"

"From what I can gather, Reggie Stewart was last seen that Saturday night. Which would suggest that was the night he was killed and buried in my vegetable plot."

"I understood he died of a heart attack."

"Brought on by a brutal beating."

"And you think I had something to do with it?"

"I am simply trying to eliminate possibilities."

"With respect, your ladyship, isn't that the job of the police?"

"Ostensibly, yes. In my position as lady of the manor, however, I feel obligated to offer my assistance in this unfortunate matter."

"I see." Henry's small eyes gleamed as he leaned back. "I can assure you, Lady Elizabeth, I am not a murderer, nor a thug who gives out thrashings. Nor would I be a part of any such atrocity. There is enough killing going on in the world right now as it is. I am a firm believer in peaceful methods of solving a problem."

"So you did have a problem to solve with Reggie Stewart?"

Henry visibly stiffened. "I have no idea what you mean."

"I'm referring to your relationship with Betty Stewart."

"Lady Elizabeth, you have gone beyond the bounds of human decency. I must ask you—"

"Are you going to deny that you were in Mrs. Stewart's house the night we arrived to inform her of her husband's death?" Elizabeth leaned forward and picked up the pipe smoldering in a large ashtray. "This does belong to you, does it not?"

Henry's face turned a deep red. "Lady Elizabeth, I—"

"It's quite all right, Henry. I believe your story." Elizabeth rose. "I don't believe you have it in you to beat a man to death. I sincerely hope, however, that you did not assist someone else in disposing of evidence."

"If you're asking if I helped Betty Stewart bury her husband," Henry said fiercely, "I can most assuredly tell you I did not."

"That's not what I was asking." Elizabeth glanced at the clock above the door. "But I appreciate your honesty." She rose, and crossed to the main door, feeling very satisfied with her little chat.

CHAPTER

❀ 10 ❀

Elizabeth's next visit was to the police station, where George sat behind the front desk, reading the newspaper. He hurriedly folded it and buried it under a stack of forms when Elizabeth entered.

"Good morning, your ladyship." He stumbled to his feet. "I was just thinking about you, I was."

"Really, George?" Elizabeth took her usual seat across from him and crossed her ankles. "I trust they were pleasant thoughts."

"Yes, m'm. They were. There's a bit in the newspaper here about the garden fete. Says here as how you're going to judge the talent contest." He unearthed the newspaper and held it out to her.

"The talent contest?" Elizabeth leaned forward to read the brief paragraph. "Well, so I am. I'm not sure what qualifications I have for judging talent, however."

"You just have to say what pleases you, m'm. That's

all." George puffed out his chest. "I have a bit of talent meself, I do."

"Really, George? I didn't know that."

"Oh, yes, m'm. I'm the best whistler in these parts. Ask anyone. They'll tell you."

Elizabeth frowned. "Whistler?"

"Yes, m'm. I can whistle. Like this." George threw back his head, pursed his lips, and emitted a shrill, ear-splitting sound that crossed Elizabeth's eyes.

"Thank you, George," she said hastily. "That's very nice, but I do think you should save your breath for the talent contest."

"Oh, right, m'm. You will bear in mind that whistling is an art form? Takes a lot of talent to stay on key, it does."

"So I noticed." She tried not to wince. "Er . . . George, I wonder if you could answer a question that's been puzzling me lately."

George leaned back and tucked his thumbs behind his lapels. "Well, your ladyship, you understand it sort of depends on what the question might be."

"Yes, quite. I was just wondering, if someone beats a man, and that man then has a heart attack and dies, would that be construed as murder?"

"Aggravated murder, I would think. Yes, m'm. If you're talking about the case of Reggie Stewart's murder, that's what the inspector is calling it."

Elizabeth stared at him in surprise. "Then you have reported it to the inspector?"

"Oh, yes, m'm. Have to do that right away, don't we? 'Course, that don't mean he's going to deal with it right away. Like he says, the body's already cold, so there's no hurry. Any clues that might have been left about, like footprints or stuff around the grave site, have been dug up or disturbed, haven't they? As for who did it, well, he's long gone by now. Right now the inspector's got another case he's working on, but he's got all the information on it, don't you worry about that."

"Have there been any further developments in the case? Other than what we already know?"

"Not to my knowledge, no." George reached for the newspaper again. "I reckon we'll just have to wait until the inspector gets around to investigating it, won't we?"

Elizabeth got up from her chair, and George rose slowly to his feet. "Do you have any ideas who might have done this, George?"

"I have lots of ideas who might have done it. That don't mean to say they did do it, though, do it?"

"You're quite right. One shouldn't jump to conclusions." She reached the door and looked back at him. "What about his wife? Do you think she's capable of beating her husband to death?"

George shrugged. "If you mean is she strong enough, I'd say it's possible. Can't say as to how her mind works, though. Not many ladies have the stomach to kill."

"I suppose it all depends on how much one has to gain."

"That would be the question, m'm. No doubt of it."

"Well, thank you, George." Elizabeth left him standing there, and ran down the steps to where she'd left her motorcycle. One more stop before she went home. She needed the afternoon to rest. Tonight she would be attending the cocktail party at the American air base, and she was determined to look her very best. It would not be easy to be with Earl and pretend indifference to his presence, but it would be worth it for the chance to spend the evening with him in his own environment.

She was looking forward to it immensely, and the prospect finally banished her depression and raised her spirits as she tootled through the village to Betty Stewart's house.

As she approached the cottage, she saw an ancient, rusty bicycle with a slightly buckled wheel leaning against the fence. She recognized it instantly. Cyril Appleby, Sitting Marsh's affable postman, used it to make his deliveries. Elizabeth often wondered how much longer the

aging postman would cling to his wobbly steed before
accepting the brand-new bicycle the local postmaster had
offered him.

Cyril stoutly maintained that his bicycle had been good
enough to carry him around the village for more than
thirty years, and he wasn't about to abandon it now for
one of those "modern jobbies."

Elizabeth smiled as she spotted Cyril ambling down the
Stewarts' garden path with his heavy postbag over his
shoulder. Closeted by her parents in the vast wasteland of
the Manor House as a child, she had considered watching
Cyril weave up the curving driveway one of the highlights
of her day.

She waved to him, then climbed off her motorcycle and
carefully straightened her skirt.

"If you've come to pay a call on Mrs. Stewart, your
ladyship, she ain't home," Cyril informed her, jerking a
thumb past his ear. "Probably out shopping. They usually
are this time of day."

"Ah, well, it can wait. Thank you, Cyril."

She was about to climb aboard her motorcycle again
when Cyril said mournfully, "Awful, that, about Reggie.
Wonder who's going to deliver the coal now?"

"I imagine they'll find someone before the winter
comes." Elizabeth straightened her hat, which, in spite of
its anchors of pins and a silk scarf, had slipped over her
ear. "Did you know Mr. Stewart well? I was under the
impression he didn't have many friends."

"I don't know as you could call us friends, your ladyship. More like acquaintances, I'd say. We went to work
on the bus together every morning. I have to say, it was
a shock to hear about him being dead and buried like that.
Nasty business. Do they know who did it?"

"Not as far as I know. When was the last time you saw
Mr. Stewart?"

Cyril scratched his head. "It was a week ago last Friday.
We sat next to each other on the bus. I looked for him
on the Monday morning, and he wasn't there. A few days

later I heard about him being found buried in your Victory Gardens. Must have been a shock for you."

"It was, indeed." Elizabeth grasped the handlebars of her motorcycle and prepared to swing her leg as elegantly as possible over the saddle.

"Well, at least the poor bugger won't have to go and fight for his country. I just dropped off his Army papers. Too bad he didn't think of doing that sooner, or he might still be alive."

Elizabeth lowered her leg again. "Mr. Stewart was called up into the Army?"

Cyril nodded. "Must have volunteered. He kept talking about doing it, but I never thought he would. Didn't seem like the type of person who would willingly risk his life for his country. Just goes to show you never know."

"Indeed you don't," Elizabeth agreed.

"Well, what do you know! There's Betty Stewart coming down the road. Must have just got off the bus." His words were nearly drowned out by the roar of the bus rumbling by in a cloud of smelly smoke. "Reckon I'll be off now," he said, as the noise of the engine faded into the distance. He tipped his hat at Elizabeth and mounted his bicycle.

She watched him wobble off and wave to Betty Stewart as he passed her. Loaded down with two heavy shopping bags, she managed to return his wave, but her attention was fixed on Elizabeth. A frown marred her face as she approached. She responded to Elizabeth's cheery greeting in a surly tone that clearly indicated her reluctance to speak. "Were you waiting for me, Lady Elizabeth?"

"Not exactly." Elizabeth gave her a friendly smile. "I was passing by and stopped to speak to Cyril. But since you're here now, I was wondering if you'd heard anything about the things that were stolen from your house."

Betty sighed and set her shopping bags on the ground. "Not a word." She flexed her arms, as if easing tired muscles. "Nor do I expect to hear anything. Whoever took them has got rid of them by now, I shouldn't wonder."

"Well, you'd certainly recognize the photo frame if you saw it again. Maybe you should look in the pawnshop in North Horsham. I understand the photograph meant a great deal to your husband. You must be anxious to get it back."

Betty Stewart shrugged. "What's gone is gone, that's what I say." She glanced up the path at her front door. "I'd ask you in, your ladyship, but I'm really not prepared for visitors at this moment."

"That's quite all right. I was just off myself." Elizabeth grasped the handlebars of her motorcycle again. "Oh, Cyril happened to mention that he'd delivered some Army papers for Mr. Stewart. I thought I should prepare you. In view of your husband's death, receiving something like that must come as an unpleasant surprise."

Betty's face was blank when she answered. "Thank you, your ladyship. I appreciate that."

"It appears that your husband did volunteer for the Army, after all."

"That's what he said he was going to do when he left the house. 'Course, he'd been saying it for weeks. Said it so many times I didn't believe him."

"And you didn't see him again after he left the house that day?"

Betty's chin came up, and her eyes blazed with sudden fire. "I didn't kill him, Lady Elizabeth, if that's what you're asking. I know what everyone in the village is thinking. Even Henry thought so at first. I—" She broke off, her bottom lip caught between her teeth.

"I've talked to Henry." Elizabeth straightened. "He said he didn't help you bury your husband. A rather unfortunate choice of words, under the circumstances."

Resentment burned in Betty's face. "Lady Elizabeth, Henry and I might have fancied each other, but it was all innocent. Henry isn't the kind of person who would mess around with another man's wife. Reggie and I didn't get along—everyone knows that—but I didn't kill him. I'd swear to that on the Bible. I was brought up strict Catholic. I couldn't divorce Reggie. I certainly wouldn't have killed him. As for Henry, he wouldn't hurt a fly. And he knows I didn't kill Reggie now. He swears he does. Whatever he said to you must have just come out wrong, that's all."

There was a ring of truth in her voice that Elizabeth found difficult to ignore. "That's entirely possible," she said slowly.

"What's more," Betty said with defiance, "if it comes right down to it, I can prove I didn't kill my husband."

Elizabeth stared at her. "Really? How?"

Betty looked as if she'd like to cut out her tongue. "It's nothing, m'm. I'd rather not say at this time."

"Whatever it is, it might be of some help to the constables in their investigation."

"No, it's not going to help nobody." She picked up her bags again. "If you'll excuse me, m'm, I should get my shopping in the house."

Frustrated, Elizabeth had to let it go. She watched Betty trudge up the path to her front door before straddling the saddle of her motorcycle. Her mind raced with possibilities while she rode back through the town. Was Betty with Henry in North Horsham that Saturday night? Was that the proof she was talking about? If so, then she certainly wouldn't want to talk about it. But if that were so, why would Henry have thought Betty might have killed her husband?

Then again, it was by no means certain exactly when Reggie Stewart had died. All anyone knew was that he'd last been seen on that Saturday night, and no one had seen him after that.

Maybe, Elizabeth thought, as she roared up the hill to the manor, it would be a good idea if she rang the doctor and asked for his opinion on how long Reggie had been dead when he was discovered. Not that it would tell her that much more.

There just didn't seem to be any way to find out exactly what happened after Fred Bickham and Reggie Stewart left the pub together. Which reminded her of something else she had to do. Somehow she had to persuade Scotland Yard to track down Fred Bickham for her. It seemed unlikely, after what Alfie had told her, that Fred had gone to Ireland. The question was, where had he gone, and how much chance did she have of getting the money he owed her?

By the time she arrived home, her head was buzzing so hard with her chaotic thoughts that she decided the best thing to do was sleep on it all. Nothing was to be gained by worrying too much about it now. Perhaps, if she gave her brain a rest, she'd be able to tie up everything she knew and make some sense of it.

She couldn't help thinking that in the tangle of information she had, there was a common thread winding through it, and if she could find that thread and give it a tug, everything would fall into place.

Right now, however, her head ached with the effort of sorting everything out. She had the afternoon to rest and regain her energy before the cocktail party that evening. And that's exactly what she was going to do.

"I want to see him before I leave, and I'm not going home until they let me in there." Polly stood by the side of her hospital bed with her arms crossed and glared at her mother. "I don't care if you do have a taxi waiting."

"Do you know how much it's costing me to have a taxi waiting outside?" Edna glared at her daughter. "What's so important you have to see this man right now? Why can't it wait until you're better and you can come back on the bus to see him?"

"The nurse told me he might not get better. I have to see him." Unable to bear the thought, Polly felt her eyes brim with tears.

"I don't know why you're making such a fuss, that I don't. The man nearly killed you."

"It wasn't his fault. The man on the bicycle was in the middle of the road."

"Well, thank God your Yank had the presence of mind to miss him. Still, he almost killed you in the process."

Polly started crying in earnest. "He might *die,* Ma . . . I've *got* to see him. I can't go home without seeing him. I just can't."

Edna stared at her daughter, then let out her breath in an explosive sigh. "Oh, very well. But make it snappy. That taxi is costing me good money."

"Thanks, Ma!" Polly rushed to the door, then halted as the room started spinning again.

"Take it easy, my girl. The doctor said to move slowly. You should be in a wheelchair, that's what I think."

Polly shook her head to clear it. "I'll be fine, Ma. Wait for me in the taxi. I'll only be a minute, I promise."

"You'd better be. Think I'm made of money, you do."

Polly left her mother to gather up her things and walked as quickly as she dared down the corridor to the lift. A few minutes later she was at the nurses' desk on the next floor. "I came to see Squadron Leader Cutter," she said, when the nurse looked up. "I'm Polly Barnett, the one who was with him in the accident. I'm leaving the hospital now, but I wanted to see him before I left." She put her whole heart into her eyes. "Please?"

"Well, I'm not supposed to—"

"Oh, please. I won't be a minute, I promise."

"He's still unconscious. He won't know you're there."

"He'll know." Polly held up a finger. "Just one minute?"

The nurse looked up and down the corridor. "Well, all right. But make it quick. If the sister catches you—"

"She won't catch me." Polly beamed her thanks. "I'll be right back." She hurried to the door the nurse had indicated and quietly opened it.

The still figure on the bed didn't move as she crept closer. His entire face was hidden behind bandages, with just a space for his nose and mouth. He was so motionless that for a dreadful moment she thought he was dead.

Then, with a rush of relief, she saw the slight rise and fall of his chest beneath the white covers.

She covered his cold hand with hers, and gently squeezed it. "It's me, Polly," she whispered. "I just wanted you to know I'm all right. I'm going home today. But I'll be back as soon as I can, so you'd better hurry up and wake up so we can talk when I come back. There's lots we need to talk about."

Her throat hurt, and she swallowed. "I'm sorry I didn't tell you how old I was when we met, Sam. I know I should have done, but I knew you were older than me, and you were sitting there in that jeep looking so handsome, and I knew lots of girls would be after you, and if I told you how old I was, you wouldn't have gone out with me. I was going to tell you, honest I was. But it's going to be all right, Sam, really it is. I'm sixteen now, and that's grown up, and I'll be seventeen in another few months, so it's going to be all right. . . ."

Her voice broke, and she struggled to hold back the sobs. He looked so helpless lying there. If only she could see his face, and give him a quick kiss. If only he'd open his eyes, just to let her know everything was going to be all right again.

She leaned forward and gently laid her forehead on his chest. "I love you, Sam. Just don't die, all right? I couldn't bear to live if you die now. Please, don't die."

The door opened behind her, and a voice hissed, "Sister's coming. You've got to go."

Polly lifted her head, kissed the tips of her fingers and laid them gently against the bandaged cheek. "I'll be back, Sam. Wake up soon."

She managed to hold her tears until she was in the lift again, then she bawled like a baby, much to the obvious concern of an orderly who rode down with her. By the time she joined her mother, who waited impatiently at the door of the taxi, she'd composed herself enough to get through the ride home without crying again.

But in the privacy of her bedroom, she gave in to the

misery engulfing her. If Sam died, her world would end, too. She would go to her grave knowing that his last conscious moments on earth were spent being angry at her. That was something she couldn't bear to live with. If Sam died, the only way she could make up with him was to meet him in heaven. If Sam died, she would have to give up her own life, too. That's all there was to it.

CHAPTER

🎀 11 🎀

Elizabeth spent a great deal of thought on her outfit for the cocktail party and finally settled on basic black with a double string of pearls left to her by her mother. One of the few items of jewelry Elizabeth hadn't sold to help cover the debts left by her gambler ex-husband.

She left her hair unpinned, and used a touch of rouge to add color to her pale cheeks. In spite of the summer sun, the brims of her hats continuously shaded her face. Her mother had always maintained that too much sunshine made a woman appear unfeminine and unrefined. After all, appearance was everything.

Elizabeth smiled at the thought. Nowadays that seemed to be more important to her than ever. Especially now that she had a reason to primp a little.

Her hand shook as she applied the merest dash of red lipstick. It had been quite some time since she had attended anything as elegant as a cocktail party. She was really looking forward to it. She studied her image in the mirror with a critical eye, aware that the prospect would not be nearly so inviting were it not for the anticipation of spending the entire evening as the guest of Major Earl Monroe.

He was waiting for her in the hallway when she descended the stairs. As always, the first sight of him, so tall and handsome in his dress uniform, churned her stomach so badly she was certain she was about to dispose of her afternoon tea in a most unbecoming manner.

"You look absolutely charming," he told her as she advanced a careful step at a time, for fear of turning an ankle on her slim heels.

"Thank you, and I'd like to return the compliment." She smiled up at him, feeling as giddy as a young girl. "Are we ready to go?"

He offered her his arm with a slight bow of his head. "Your carriage awaits, ma'am."

A gruff voice spoke from the shadows, startling them both. "I trust your father is aware of your intentions, young lady?"

Earl jerked his head around. "What the . . . ?"

Elizabeth peered at Martin, who was shuffling out from behind the library door. "For heaven's sake, Martin, what are you doing lurking about like that?"

Martin almost managed to straighten his body. His voice rang with indignation. "Lurking *about*, madam? I never lurk. I was merely waiting for you to appear in order to open the door for you, as is my duty." He eyed Earl with a skeptical frown. "I trust your intentions are honorable, Major?"

Embarrassed, Elizabeth started to protest, but Earl cut in. "Perfectly honorable, Martin. I'm just escorting Lady Elizabeth to a cocktail party at the base. All very innocent and aboveboard, I promise you."

Martin seemed unappeased. "Then, sir, where is your chaperone, may I ask?"

Earl appeared at a loss for an answer to that. Elizabeth

stepped forward, into the light of the crystal chandelier. "Look at me, Martin. Do you really think I need a chaperone?"

Martin blinked his watery blue eyes. "Every decent young woman needs a chaperone, madam. Ask your father. He would not allow you to compromise your reputation this way. I'm sure he will be most displeased when he hears about this."

"He's not going to hear anything," Elizabeth said firmly. "My father is dead, Martin. Surely you remember that. He's dead, and so is my mother. I am a divorced woman. There isn't much I can do that would besmirch my image any more than it is already. In which case, I think we can dispense with the chaperone, don't you?"

Martin, who had listened to her somewhat terse statements without blinking, nodded rather sadly. "Very well, madam. If you say so."

"I do say so. Now kindly open the door and let us be on our way."

She saw Earl hide a grin as Martin obediently opened the door with a great deal of straining and puffing, then stood back to direct a dark look at the major. "I shall hold you personally accountable for the lady's welfare," he muttered.

Earl stooped to whisper in his ear words that Elizabeth couldn't catch. Whatever he'd said, it seemed to satisfy Martin, who nodded affably as he began the task of closing the massive door. His last words drifted out to them as they descended the steps. "Do have a good time, madam."

"Just as long as you don't besmirch your image," Earl teased, as they walked down the steps. "Is that really true?"

"Is what true?"

"That being divorced is such a crime?"

"For a woman here in England, anyway, it's considered quite shocking. Particularly if one happens to be the lady of the manor. There's a stigma attached to the word 'divorcée.' No matter who's at fault. Isn't it the same in your country?"

"I guess so. I hadn't really thought about it."

"Grossly unfair, of course."

"Don't you ever get tired of having to uphold that kind of image?"

"Constantly." She sighed. "There are times when I'd like to forget who I am, and just do whatever I feel like doing, without having to worry about what people think."

Their footsteps echoed across the courtyard, and one of the dogs in the kitchen barked when Earl slammed the door of the jeep. "What was it you whispered to Martin?" Elizabeth asked, as she settled herself on the front seat.

Earl swung himself in next to her and fired the ignition. Above the roar of the engine she was almost positive she heard him say, "I promised him that if you were compromised in any way, I'd make an honest woman of you."

Speechless, she pulled a silk scarf from her pocket, draped it around her head, and tied it under her chin. The jeep rolled forward in the clean, fresh air of the summer night. She became acutely aware of the sweet smell of newly cut grass and lifted her face to enjoy the damp breeze from the ocean.

They were almost at the end of the drive when Earl said, his voice teasing, "What, no comment?"

Elizabeth struggled to regain her composure. "I was thinking," she said carefully, "that under the circumstances, you would find it difficult to keep that promise."

"Reckon I would, but since you're unlikely to be compromised by me—or anyone else, for that matter—I figured I was safe."

She thought that over for a while. "How do you know?" she asked at last.

He sounded wary when he answered. "How do I know what?"

"That I won't be compromised by anyone else?"

His pause was unnerving. By the time he finally answered, she was on pins and needles, wishing she hadn't pursued this dangerous line of conversation. "You are an exceptionally strong woman, Elizabeth. I can't see you allowing yourself to be compromised by anyone. Whatever you choose to do, it will be only after you've considered every angle and have fully convinced yourself it's the right thing to do. I admire that and I respect it. I'm not sure I could be that honorable."

Little bumps began popping out all over her arms. "Given the right circumstances," she said, with reckless daring, "I'm not sure I could be, either."

"Well, now, that's an interesting thought."

Her lungs hurt with the effort to breathe normally. She would never know if they were talking about the same thing. Nor dared she ask. But somehow she was certain that for the rest of her life, she would never forget this night—the wind in her face, her body alive with the excitement of something magical just out of reach and the tantalizing possibility of its drawing ever closer.

She wasn't sure if she was relieved or disappointed when Earl changed the subject. "In all the excitement," he said, as they turned onto the coast road, "I almost forgot. I've got some good news."

Eagerly she turned to him. "Sam Cutter?"

"Right. He's out of the coma. The doc thinks he's on the mend, though it will take some time."

"Oh, Earl, that *is* good news." She gave his arm a little squeeze with both her hands. "Polly will be ecstatic."

"I'm not so sure about that." Earl's voice sobered. "Not when she gets the whole story."

Dismayed, Elizabeth peered at his shadowed face. "What's wrong? He's not crippled, is he?"

"Not as far as I know. He's a tough guy, and the doc seems to think he'll be good as new. Except. . . ."

She waited with dread for him to finish the sentence. When he didn't, she prompted, "Except for what? What is it?"

"It's his face." Earl sighed. "Sam was a good-looking guy. It's gonna be tough on him now."

"Oh, no." Elizabeth sank back in her seat. "Will he be badly scarred?"

"The right side of his face was ground into the road. Took most of his cheek and broke a couple of bones. He'll mend, but they won't get all the gravel out, and the doc says his face will probably be sunken in on that side. The scars will be pretty obvious."

Elizabeth's excitement faded at this disturbing news. "Poor Sam. He's still so young."

"The good side of it is, they saved the sight in that eye. Other than the scars, he'll soon be as fit as the rest of us."

"Will they send him home?"

"That'll be up to the Army medics to decide. If all goes well with him, they may just patch him up and send him back up in his plane. It's what he wants, according to the doc."

"Then let's hope that's what they'll do."

"What about Polly? She might change her mind about him when she sees him. I sure hope she doesn't. That young lady could really help him get through this. If she turns her back on him now, he might never look at himself in a mirror again."

"I understand what you're saying." Elizabeth touched his arm. "Don't worry, Earl. I've seen Polly's face when she talks about Sam. She adores him. She'll stand by him. Actually, I was going to talk to her about that. I don't think her mother is aware of their relationship. I was going to insist that Polly tell her mother the truth. Now that this has happened, Edna just might be able to understand Sam's need, and accept the fact that her sixteen-year-old daughter is in love with a man almost ten years older."

"Polly's only sixteen?" Earl whistled softly through his teeth. "That does put a different light on things, I reckon."

"I don't see why. I think it's up to the individuals concerned. When two people love each other, it's amazing the obstacles they can overcome if they truly want to be together."

"Well, well, well. The lady is a liberal after all. You

surprise me, Elizabeth. I had you pegged as a true conservative."

"Me?" Elizabeth had to laugh. "In some things I have to be, I suppose. But as I've said, underneath this proper, conventional image of the lady of the manor lives a rebel who has been known to rear her militant head every once in a while."

"Don't I know it." He laughed—a rich sound that warmed her blood. That warmth stayed with her throughout the evening. Though she didn't have much chance to talk with him again, it was enough for her to know he was close by while she exchanged pleasantries with the officers and local dignitaries.

Several times throughout the evening she met his gaze briefly from across the room, and the smiles he sent her made her feel as if she could conquer the world single-handed.

Although she enjoyed tasting the unusual hors d'oeuvres and listening to the various accents against a background of recorded band music, she was eager for the evening to end and allow her to be alone with the major once more.

At last they were speeding back along the coast road, exchanging amusing anecdotes about the various people who had attended the party.

They were almost home before she remembered what she'd wanted to ask him. "I've been asked to judge the talent contest at the garden fete on Saturday," she said, as they drove up the hill toward the manor. "I don't suppose you'd care to give me a hand? I'm not terribly good at this sort of thing. I feel awful when I can't choose everyone to be a winner."

He chuckled. "I can believe that. I'm not sure I'd be any better at it. As far as I'm concerned, anyone who stands up and performs in front of an audience deserves a prize for sheer guts."

"Exactly. But perhaps between the two of us we could at least come to some kind of decision."

"Okay, I'll see what I can do. I can't promise anything, though."

Well satisfied, she accepted that. He'd do his best to be there, she knew, and that was enough for her. "I had a wonderful time," she told him when he drew up in front of the manor. "I can't remember when I've enjoyed an evening quite so much."

Although she couldn't see his expression, his voice teased her once more. "Are you telling me that this tops the night I rescued you from a brawling mob at the Town Hall Massacre?"

She had to laugh. "That *was* rather a fiasco. I had really hoped that a dance at the town hall would help improve the relationship between the British and Americans in the village. I failed dismally, I'm afraid."

"It wasn't your best idea. But the cricket match turned out all right."

"Well, at least it wasn't a disaster. But things really haven't changed that much. There are still fights at the pub, skirmishes on the streets, and a general feeling of animosity toward the Americans. Among the men in particular."

"I reckon there isn't much we can do to change that. Any time you have a bunch of strangers coming into town and making passes at your women, you're going to get sore at them."

"Especially when they are more attractive, more exciting, and better paid than the average British soldier. I suppose it must be frightfully frustrating for them."

"If I were in their shoes, I'd be out there busting their faces, too."

It was her turn to laugh. "Why, Major, I was under the impression that you were a pacifist."

"Wherever did you get that idea?"

"I . . . don't know. Just an opinion I'd formed, I suppose." Unsettled, she politely smothered a yawn. "I had better go in or Martin will be out here with a big stick, ready to defend my honor."

Earl chuckled and swung himself out of his seat. In a few quick strides he rounded the rear of the jeep and opened her door for her. "You can tell Martin your honor is still intact."

"I'll do that." She smiled up at him, wishing she could see well enough to read his eyes. "Thank you, Earl. It was a delightful evening. One I shall remember for a long time."

"You're entirely welcome. It was my pleasure." Standing close to her, he touched the peak of his cap with his fingers. "Good night, Elizabeth."

Aware of him watching her, she climbed the steps. She was almost at the top when he said softly, "Exciting and attractive, huh?"

Smiling, she turned to look at his shadowy figure. "Most assuredly, Major."

He didn't answer, but she knew he was grinning as he returned to the jeep and noisily drove away.

Still smiling, she reached for the bell pull, then snatched her hand back. It was late, and both Martin and Violet were no doubt fast asleep. Hoping that Violet hadn't locked the kitchen door, as she'd suggested, Elizabeth made her way around the massive stone wall of the manor and hurried past the greenhouses to the kitchen yard.

To her relief, the door opened at the turn of the handle, and she stepped into the warm kitchen, blinking to adjust her sight to the dim light of the furnace. As she did so, she heard a scuffling sound from the larder, the door of which stood open.

Her immediate thought was that rats were responsible, and she looked around for the broom that Violet kept standing by the fireplace. Crossing the room, she snatched it up and advanced on the larder. At least that would solve one of the mysteries. If there were rats in there, that would no doubt answer the question of the missing food.

With her foot she edged the door open wider. Something had been rummaging around in there, that much was obvious. On the shelf below the window several packages and a bag of flour had been overturned. A tin of soup lay on its side, still rolling gently back and forth.

After inspecting the minuscule room for vermin, Elizabeth rested the broomstick against the wall. She hadn't really expected to see a rat in there. Rats might well be bold and adventurous when hungry and seeking food, but she had yet to see one that could open a window and climb out of it to escape.

At breakfast the next morning, Elizabeth was disconcerted when Martin, after much wheezing and groaning with the effort of seating himself, inquired, "I trust that blasted American behaved himself last night, madam?"

Violet spun around so sharply her elbow whipped a saucepan off the counter. The dogs barked and rushed around as the pot bounced and rolled across the tiled floor. By the time order had been restored, Elizabeth had collected herself enough to meet Violet's sharp gaze without flinching.

"What blasted American?" the housekeeper demanded, bringing two bowls of porridge to the table. "What's the old goat talking about now?"

Before Elizabeth could answer, Martin said peevishly, "Porridge again? When are we going to have eggs and bacon and sausage and tomatoes and fried potatoes and fried bread—"

"Be quiet, you old fool," Violet snapped. "You're making my stomach rumble. You know you don't get all that until Sunday breakfast."

"Isn't this Sunday?" Martin peered at Elizabeth over the top of his glasses. "Didn't I see you leaving with that American for a social appointment last night, madam?"

"You did, Martin." Elizabeth met Violet's hard stare. "I did mention I was going to a cocktail party with Major Monroe, didn't I?"

"No, you didn't. You said you had an engagement, but you didn't say where."

"Oh." Elizabeth tried to sound innocent. "I thought I'd told you where I was going."

"It must have been Saturday night if you were socializing," Martin muttered.

"People socialize on a weeknight sometimes, Martin." Elizabeth avoided Violet's gaze.

"Not in my day they didn't." Martin dug his spoon into his porridge and began pushing it around in circles. "The weekdays are for working. The weekends are for socializing."

"People who have secrets usually have something to hide," Violet said meaningfully, ignoring Martin's comments.

"I have nothing to hide." Elizabeth lifted her chin. She longed to tell Violet it was none of her business where she went and with whom. She knew quite well, however, that if she did so, her housekeeper would sulk for at least a day or two, and make life unbearable until she got over it.

Since the death of her parents, Elizabeth had tolerated Violet's attempts to substitute for them, but sometimes the housekeeper overstepped the boundaries. Elizabeth had to admit she was uncommonly sensitive about her relationship with Earl Monroe, but there was a limit to what she would allow as far as her housekeeper's special privileges were concerned.

Fortunately, Violet must have read the warning in her expression. "I hope you had a good time."

"I had a very enjoyable evening, thank you. The major was very gracious, and I met some very interesting people on the base."

"Glad to hear it." Violet stomped back to the stove, then, without turning around, muttered, "You know I worry about what happens to you. There's no one else to worry about you now."

Instantly softening, Elizabeth said quickly, "I know, Violet. But I'm a big girl. I can take care of myself."

Still with her back to her, Violet said, "I just don't want you to make another big mistake."

"Neither do I. So trust me. All right?" Deliberately, Elizabeth changed the subject. "Did you find anything else missing from the larder this morning?"

"I haven't looked yet." Violet spun around and glared at Martin. "Why, has he been thieving in there again?"

Martin looked up in protest, but before he could speak, Elizabeth cut in. "No, it's not Martin. I doubt if he could climb out of the larder window."

Violet's thin, straggly eyebrows nearly disappeared into her frizzy hairline. "Window?"

"I heard something in the larder when I came home last night. You didn't leave the window open in there, did you?"

"Of course not." Violet sent a nervous glance toward the larder. "I never leave it open. Too many wasps and flies around this time of year."

"That's what I thought. Whoever was raiding our larder last night escaped through the window."

Looking alarmed now, Violet lowered her voice. "It hasn't got anything to do with that poor man they found buried in the gardens, has it?"

"I shouldn't think so. I can't imagine what connection there could possibly be between a murderer and a common thief."

"Well, it's just that robbery at Betty Stewart's house, too. Bit of a coincidence, if you ask me. Has anyone else been robbed?"

"I really don't know." Elizabeth glanced at Martin, who was scraping the bottom of his bowl as if he intended to put a hole in it. "Perhaps I should ask George about that. I have to go into the village today, in any case. I want to take another look at the cottage Fred Bickham rented. If I'm going to rent it again, I need to see what needs doing to it."

"Good-for-nothing sod, that Fred is. Taking off like that without paying his rent money."

Violet went on muttering, but Elizabeth wasn't listening. She was thinking about the fact that Fred and Reggie had left the pub together, and neither of them had been seen again, until Reggie's body was discovered buried in her Victory Gardens.

She was also thinking about the personal possessions Fred had left behind. She had to wonder if Fred *had* gone to Ireland, as he'd said in his note, or if the reason he hadn't paid his rent was because he couldn't. Perhaps Reggie wasn't the only person to die that night. In which case, while she was at the cottage that morning, it wouldn't hurt to look around a bit more thoroughly.

Not that she expected to find Fred's body, of course. She surely would have seen him had he been there the last time she paid a visit. There was, however, a slim chance she would find a clue to what had happened to him. It was becoming increasingly clear that something significant must have happened. One man was dead, another was missing. Unless Fred was found alive, at this point it seemed doubtful that anyone would ever know what evil had befallen those two men after the Tudor Arms closed its doors on that fateful night.

CHAPTER 12

Polly's heart thumped with anxiety as she tapped on the door of Sam's room. A muffled sound answered her, and she took it to be an invitation. Sending up a silent prayer, she pushed open the door and went in.

She wasn't sure what she was expecting, but he didn't look much different from the last time she'd seen him. Except that a little more of his face was visible today. The nurse had warned her that he wasn't in a very good mood. She could tell that by the one eye she could see.

"Hi, Sam." Her lips quivered, and she had to take a deep breath before she could go on. "You're looking better today."

His mouth looked bruised on one side, and he spoke as if it hurt him to move his lips. "What are you doing here?"

It wasn't the welcome she was hoping for, and she clenched her fingers to keep the tears from spurting. She'd promised herself she wouldn't make a fool of herself in front of him. She just hadn't realized how hard it was going to be. "I came to see you, didn't I?"

"How did you get here?"

"I came on the bus."

"I thought you were supposed to be in bed."

"I was. I came to tell you I was sorry."

"For what?"

"For lying about my age. For making you angry." She swallowed, praying she wouldn't cry. "It was my fault you crashed the jeep. If you hadn't been so cross with me. . . ."

"Cut it out," Sam said gruffly. "I was the one driving. It wasn't your fault. Are you okay? They said you had a concussion."

"Just a slight one. I'm all right now. But it was my fault, really. You were angry with me."

"I was angry at myself, for being such a sucker. I should have known better than to get messed up with a kid."

The pain cut so deep she almost cried out. "I'm not a kid, Sam. I'm not any different than I was before I told you. You didn't think I was a kid then."

"I didn't know how old you were then."

She shook her head in bewilderment. "Why does that make any difference? It doesn't change the person I am."

Sam turned his head so she couldn't see his eye. "It changes everything."

In spite of her best efforts, tears began running down her cheeks. She swiped at them with the back of her hand. "I love you, Sam. I love you. I thought you loved me."

"What does a kid like you know about love anyway?"

"I'm not a kid!" She was sobbing now, helpless against the tide of misery that engulfed her. "Sam, why are you doing this? Why are you being so horrible to me?"

He turned his head so fiercely that he groaned. She put out a hand to touch him, but the look in his eye stopped her. "Look, it's over. Don't you understand? Go home,

Polly. Find yourself another boyfriend and forget you ever knew me."

"I c-a-a-n't. I'll never forget you. I—" She slapped a hand over her mouth as the door opened behind her.

A sharp voice demanded, "What's all this?"

Polly's heart sank as she recognized the commanding tone. "Good morning, Sister," she said weakly.

The nurse glared at her. "What are you doing upsetting my patient? He's supposed to be resting quietly. And you were supposed to be resting at home. What are you doing here?"

"I just came to visit him. . . ." Her voice trailed off as the nurse took a firm hold of her arm.

"Well, child, the visit is over. I want you to go straight home and get into bed. The doctor was quite specific about you staying in bed for at least two more days. He won't be very happy when I tell him you were here." She tugged Polly over to the door, ignoring her attempts to speak to Sam. "Come along, child. Leave this man in peace."

Reaching the door, Polly twisted her head. "Sam, please . . ."

His face was turned away from her. "Go home, Polly. Just go home."

There was nothing she could do but allow the sister to pull her out into the corridor. The tears filled her eyes and blurred her vision, and the cold, dark hole in her heart was growing bigger by the minute.

The sister must have felt sorry for her. She patted her shoulder and said briskly, "A nice cup of tea, that's what you need. Come with me, and I'll get one for you. Then you must go home and go to bed. Promise me?"

Polly nodded, the effort almost too much for her. What did it matter what she did anymore? She'd lost Sam. The only man she could ever, ever love. There'd be no house in Hollywood, no swimming pool, no fancy clothes. But far worse than any of that, there'd be no more Sam. It was too much to bear. Somehow it was worse than if he'd died.

She stumbled along by the sister's side, unable to hold up her head to see where they were going. She vaguely remembered someone putting a mug of tea in her hand. She must have drunk it, though she didn't remember tasting it. Nor did she remember leaving the hospital. All she knew was that she was sitting on the bus going back to Sitting Marsh, and that she would never, ever smile again.

"Lady Elizabeth!" Martin exclaimed, as Elizabeth was about to open the front door. "Whatever are you doing?"

"I'm going out, Martin." Elizabeth smiled at him. "I shan't be long."

"Well, you must allow me to open the door for you. Shall I call for the carriage to be brought around?"

"Um, no, thank you, Martin." Elizabeth drew on her gloves. "I'm taking the motorcycle."

Martin gave a sniff of disapproval as he tugged on the heavy iron latch. "Well, I suppose it's better than that blasted noisy machine those Americans drive around. Though if you want my opinion, a carriage is far more fitting for a lady of the manor."

"That may well be. Now that we have no horses, however, a carriage might be just a tiny bit impractical, don't you think?"

"No horses?" Martin blinked at her above his spectacles. "Where the devil did they go?"

"We sold them, Martin."

"Sold them?"

"Every one of them, I'm afraid."

"What a blow. No more horses. Your sisters will be very disappointed."

Elizabeth paused in the act of stepping outside. "My sisters? I don't have any sisters, Martin. I am an only child, remember?"

"Yes, madam. But you have sisters now. Three of them. I've seen them."

Elizabeth stared at him. "Where did you see them?"

"In the great hall. They were talking to your father. I couldn't hear what he was saying to them, of course, but I saw them quite clearly. One of them had beautiful long, wavy hair, just like you did when you were that age."

"That couldn't possibly have been my father, Martin. You know very well he's been dead for three years."

"So you keep telling me, madam." Martin shook his head back and forth. "So you keep telling me. You don't have to worry, I shan't tell anyone I've seen him. I'm sure there's a very good reason why we have to pretend he'd dead. Just don't tell those blasted Americans. They'll blab it all over town."

Elizabeth sighed. "Don't worry, Martin. I'll keep quiet if you promise to do the same."

Martin tapped the side of his nose with his finger. "Mum's the word, madam."

She hurried outside into a damp, misty morning, which might well have accounted for the shivers chasing up and down her spine. They couldn't possibly be due to the uneasy feeling Martin had given her. After all, *she* knew there were no such things as ghosts. Martin was simply hallucinating again.

Even so, she couldn't rid her mind of Polly's words a couple of days earlier. *I seen them, Lady Elizabeth. Three of them. Children, they were. They flitted across the great hall by the east wing.*

She saw herself standing in the dim light of the kitchen furnace, watching a shadow slip from the room. The shivers turned to a full-blown shudder.

As she hurried across the courtyard to the stables, she did her best to shake the eerie feeling. It was nonsense, of course. The shadow in the kitchen had opened the door. A ghost would have gone through it. And ghosts did not open larder windows to climb out.

No, whoever she had seen and heard in the kitchen was as human as she was. More than likely an American officer on the prowl to satisfy his late-night hunger. She would have a word with Earl about it. Perhaps he could shed some light on the mystery.

Then again, surely one of her American officers wouldn't rob the houses in the village. That made no sense at all. It had to be coincidence.

Approaching her motorcycle, she pulled the small package Earl had given her from her pocket. She'd opened it the minute she'd reached her room the night before, and had slept with the tiny St. Christopher medal he'd given her beneath her pillow. The note with it asked her to carry the medal with her for safety on her motorcycle, and she smiled as she hung it in the sidecar. From now on, she would go nowhere without it.

On the way to the village she tried to relive the memories of the evening before, but her mind would not stop wrestling with the questions that would not let her rest. By the time she reached Fred Bickham's cottage, her head ached with the effort to sort things out.

She let herself into the musty living room, wrinkling her nose at the unpleasant smell. Her first task was to open every window in the place and get some fresh air in there. Then she pulled a notebook and pencil from her handbag and prepared to make some notes. Fred's personal belongings would have to be crated up and stored until he sent for them or she received notice of how to dispose of them. The curtains in the living room would have to be washed, as would, no doubt, the curtains in the bedrooms.

Dirty dishes still lay in the kitchen sink, and Elizabeth hastily left the room to escape the offensive odor. The stairs creaked and snapped as she climbed them, and her glove was black with dust from the banister when she reached the upstairs landing.

The door to the bedroom stood ajar, and she hesitated before poking her head in to look around. She was immensely relieved to find the room empty, even though she'd already convinced herself that she would not find Fred's dead body lying there.

She was right about the curtains; they would have to

be taken down and washed. She eyed the yellow candle-wick bedspread drawn untidily over the pillows. It still looked fairly presentable, but since she rented the cottage furnished, she would have to provide clean bedding for the new tenant.

Busily jotting notes to herself, she moved to the spare bedroom and peered inside. She would have to remove the packing cases, and if the new tenants had children, she would have to provide beds for this room.

Unbidden, a vision of three ghostly children floating across the great hall came to mind. She shook it off, and concentrated on her inspection. The next thing to do was open drawers to see if Fred had left any personal belongings.

She returned to the bedroom and began opening the drawers in the dresser. As she opened each one, the cold feeling that had unsettled her ever since she had entered the cottage deepened. It was as if Fred had never left. The drawers were full of clean underwear, in untidy piles. Socks, ties, handkerchiefs . . . everything that he would take with him if he were leaving the premises for good.

Closing the last drawer with a snap, Elizabeth faced the truth. It looked very much as if Fred Bickham did not leave the cottage for a trip to anywhere, except perhaps his grave.

Sighing, Elizabeth resigned herself to informing George of her discovery. The sooner they began the search for the missing man, the better. Although by now, as the inspector had said, the trail was probably cold.

A nasty thought occurred to Elizabeth on the way to the police station. Reggie Stewart had been found buried in John Rickett's Victory Garden. No more than two weeks after John had died. He was supposed to have died from a kidney disease. But what if something else had killed him? Or someone? Could John Rickett be another link in this strange chain of events?

Elizabeth groaned out loud as she battered her way against the wind that had roared in from the sea. The further she dug into this case, the more complicated it became. What she needed was a quiet evening in her conservatory, to sort things out in her mind. Perhaps if she jotted down everything she knew, some sense might come of it. It was certainly worth a try.

George appeared uninterested in her theory about Fred Bickham's possible death. Although he promised to pass on her opinions to the inspector, she left the police station with a strong suspicion that the search for Fred would be put on hold, along with the investigation into Reggie Stewart's death.

Plagued by the conviction that, thanks to the casualties of the war, most people had become complacent about death, she was not feeling too chipper by the time she arrived back at the manor. Even the news that Sadie Buttons would be arriving the next day failed to cheer her up.

Although she was surprised to admit it, she missed Polly's cheerful chatter, not to mention her assistance, now that the correspondence and bills were piling up on her desk.

Having polished off a rather boring meal of meat pie and mashed potatoes, she decided to pay Polly a visit before tackling the tiresome paperwork.

Polly herself opened the door, and Elizabeth was taken aback by her ravaged face. She seemed heartened, though somewhat surprised, to see her visitor, however, and led Elizabeth into the cramped living room.

"I'll put the kettle on, m'm," she announced, as Elizabeth made herself comfortable on the couch.

"Oh, no, Polly, thank you. I don't care for tea right now. Just sit down and tell me how you're feeling."

Polly picked up a pile of magazines from an armchair and dropped them on the floor. "I'm doing all right, thank you, m'm." She sank onto the chair and folded her legs beneath her. "It was awfully nice of you to come."

Elizabeth studied the wan face. Polly didn't look all right. In fact, she looked as if the troubles of the world had descended on her thin shoulders. "Well, I just wanted to tell you not to worry about coming back to work too soon."

Polly looked alarmed. "Have you got someone else doing my work? Not that Sadie Buttons, I hope. She didn't sound too clever to me." Her face changed. "Not that it's any of my business, m'm. I suppose the bills have to be paid."

Elizabeth smiled. "Please don't concern yourself, Polly. No one is doing your work, and I can take care of anything important that comes along until you're well enough to return."

"To tell you the truth, m'm, I'm going bonkers sitting around the house." To Elizabeth's dismay, Polly's face crumpled. "I need to come back to work so I don't sit around thinking about things." A big tear squeezed out and splashed down her cheek.

Elizabeth leaned forward, one hand outstretched toward the girl. "Oh, Polly, dear, what's wrong? Are you in pain? Perhaps I should ring Dr. Sheridan and ask him to take a look at you."

Polly shook her head. "No, m'm, it's not that. It's *Sam!*" The last word came out on a wail.

Elizabeth sank back on the couch. "Oh, I see." Her heart ached for the two of them. Perhaps it was too much to ask that a young girl Polly's age would be able to accept a disfigured man, no matter how fond of him she was.

"I went to the hospital to see him this morning." Polly sandwiched the words between heart-wrenching sobs.

"That wasn't too wise, my dear. The doctor was quite adamant about you resting quietly for a few days."

"I know. But I had to see him, didn't I? I just didn't expect. . . ." A burst of weeping cut off the rest of her words.

Wishing she could do something to ease the girl's pain, Elizabeth sought for words of comfort. "I suppose it must have been quite a shock. Someone should have prepared you."

Polly's sobbing ceased immediately. "You *knew*?"

"Major Monroe told me last night. I'm so sorry, my dear."

"The major knew? What did Sam do, tell everyone in the village?" Polly started sobbing again. "They'll all be laughing behind me back. Thinking what a blinking fool I've been."

Elizabeth frowned. "I don't think anyone will be laughing at you, Polly. I'm quite sure, under the circumstances, they'd feel just as badly as you do. After all, it's not a laughing matter. That young man's entire life will be affected."

"*His* life? What about mine?"

Feeling just a little bit irritated, and rather disappointed in the child, Elizabeth's voice came out a little sharper than she intended. "I'm sure you'll survive, Polly. After all, you weren't permanently disfigured. Think what it will mean to Sam Cutter to have to go through life with people staring at his face—or worse, asking him what happened to him. Some people can be so terribly ignorant about such things."

Polly's damp, red-rimmed eyes were wide in her face. "Disfigured? Sam is disfigured?"

Elizabeth felt as bewildered as Polly appeared to be. "Yes—I thought that was what we were talking about."

"Oh, flipping crikey!" Polly wiped the back of her hand across her eyes. "He never told me. No one told me. I didn't know."

"Then what . . . ?"

"Lady Elizabeth." Polly climbed slowly off the chair. "Can I ask you for a really big favor?"

"Well, I—"

"Oh, please, m'm. I wouldn't ask if it wasn't a matter of life and death. Honest. I have to see Sam. Right away. Could you take me there on your motorbike? It takes so long on the bus, and there isn't one going to North Horsham for hours."

"Polly, I really don't think—"

"Please, m'm? I'd be ever so grateful. If I could just see him today, I'll come back to work tomorrow. I promise."

Elizabeth rose to her feet. "Polly, I don't know what this is all about, but I really can't accept the responsibility of taking you back to North Horsham today. You need your rest."

Polly started to protest, but Elizabeth raised her hand. "If you're feeling better tomorrow, I'll take you there first thing in the morning—"

"Oh, thank you, m'm—"

"—providing your mother agrees that you can go."

Polly's expression turned desperate. "She'll agree, I know she will. She's just *got* to let me go."

"*And* on condition that you promise me you will stay in your bed for the rest of today." Elizabeth gestured at the magazines lying on the floor. "Take those to bed with you. They'll keep you company."

"Yes, m'm, I will. Thank you ever so much."

Heartened by the hope shining in the young girl's face, Elizabeth smiled. "Just make sure your mother gives her permission. And don't worry about coming back to work until next week. I'll be busy all weekend anyway. What with Sadie Buttons arriving and the summer fete on Saturday, I'll need bed rest myself by Sunday." She turned to go, then remembered something. "I shall be attending a funeral on Monday morning, so perhaps it might be better if you plan on working just the afternoon that day."

"Yes, m'm, I'll do that. Thank you."

Still not quite sure why she was being thanked so effusively, Elizabeth took her leave.

She was still puzzling over Polly's transformation when she sat down at her desk an hour or so later. She had put off tackling the paperwork until the last possible minute, but several overdue bills needed her attention. She pulled the pile of papers from the tray and began sorting through them.

She was almost at the bottom of the pile when she came across Fred Bickham's letter. She read it again, studying each badly scrawled word. It stated quite clearly that Fred intended living with his brother in Ireland. Yet Alfie had seemed quite sure that Fred's only living relative was a sister in Devon.

Elizabeth frowned. It shouldn't be too difficult to find Fred's sister. Perhaps she would know what happened to Fred. A vision of Fred's cottage popped into Elizabeth's mind. The bedroom. There was something about the bedroom. Something she couldn't put her finger on. . . .

Another thought struck her, and she pushed her chair away from the desk and hurried over to the filing cabinet. After a moment or two she found what she was looking for, and drew the file out. Carrying it to the desk, she flipped through it, then laid it down while she extracted a sheet of paper. It was Fred Bickham's application to rent the cottage.

After studying it for another minute or so, she reached for the letter he'd written informing her of his move to Ireland. Laying them side by side, she studied them again.

At last she straightened. It really hadn't taken an expert's opinion to convince her of what she'd begun to suspect. The second letter hadn't been written by Fred. Someone else had written the letter. Someone who knew what had happened to Fred Bickham and had gone to a lot of trouble to cover up his disappearance.

CHAPTER
✿ 13 ✿

Elizabeth was up bright and early the next morning, and after a hurried breakfast rode down to Polly's house. Edna answered the door, and had obviously been expecting her. She showed her visitor into the living room, which had been visibly tidied up since Elizabeth's visit the day before.

There was no sign of Polly, however, and Elizabeth sensed a certain disapproval in Edna's voice when she offered the inevitable cup of tea.

Elizabeth declined with her most charming smile. "I have rather a busy day today. Is Polly ready to go?"

"Not quite, your ladyship." Edna pursed her lips. "If you don't mind me asking, m'm, I'd like to know what you think of this young man Polly seems so set on."

"Well, I don't know him very well," Elizabeth admitted. "But his commanding officer speaks very highly of him."

"Ah, yes, the major."

Something in the way she said it made Elizabeth feel uncomfortable. "Is there something I should know?"

"Well, it's just that this Sam Cutter is ten years older than Polly, and he is an American, after all. You know what they say about Yanks. I just don't think Polly should be getting mixed up with someone like that. She's so young, not much more than a child, really. Her dad wouldn't like it at all, I know that."

Elizabeth drew a deep breath. "Mrs. Barnett, I understand how you feel. Truly I do. But in my experience, young girls very often find a way of doing what they want, no matter how much their parents disapprove. Sometimes they do things they shouldn't, simply *because* their parents disapprove. A way of establishing their independence, I suppose."

"She's too young to have that kind of independence," Edna muttered. "Sometimes parents have to do things to protect their children."

"I've always found Polly to be a sensible and strong-willed young woman. I'm sure she's quite capable of taking care of herself. There comes a time when we have to trust people to do the right thing."

Edna's expression hardened. "It's not Polly I don't trust."

Elizabeth hesitated, then said quietly, "Mrs. Barnett, forgive me for speaking bluntly, but there's something you should know. Sam Cutter's face was disfigured in the accident. He's going to need all the support he can get to accept that. Polly could help a lot. The major believes that Sam will recover enough to return to his duties. If so . . . well . . . you know his chances of surviving the rest of the war. I would say those two young people are entitled to any happiness they can find in the next few months, wouldn't you?"

Edna chewed on her lip for a moment, then finally nodded. "If you put it like that, m'm, I don't see how I can stop our Polly from seeing him. I just don't want her heart broken, that's all."

"There are always broken hearts in wartime." Elizabeth rose to her feet. "We have to accept that, and hope the experience helps us to grow into better people because of it."

"I reckon you're right at that." Edna crossed the room to the door. "I'll tell Polly you're waiting for her."

Moments later Polly arrived in the doorway, her face wreathed in smiles. She looked so much better that Elizabeth had a hard time remembering her blotchy face and puffy eyes of the day before.

"I don't know how you swung it, your ladyship," Polly said, as she eased herself into the sidecar of Elizabeth's motorcycle, "but I'm ever so glad you're on my side. I didn't think me mum was ever going to let me see Sam."

"I only hope you can settle whatever differences you have with him. I don't need my secretary moping around the office with a long face next week."

"Well, I don't know if he's going to listen to me, m'm. But I'm not going to leave him until I have my say. He wants to break up with me, but I know it's because he thinks I won't want him with his face all banged up. Crikey, there are women out there who have men coming back from the war with arms and legs missing, or their faces all burned up and looking really horrible. They don't stop loving them just because they don't look the same. And I'll never, never stop loving Sam. I've got to make him believe that."

The wind made it impossible to have a conversation on the ride to North Horsham, but Elizabeth's heart glowed with admiration for the young girl at her side. Polly might be young, but she had the heart and soul of a woman far beyond her years. One could only hope that she would survive the heartache of loving such a man; perhaps the miracle would happen, and Polly would find lasting happiness with her Sam. At least she had hope. That was more than so many had in these troubled times.

Elizabeth left Polly at the hospital and visited the shops in the High Street for an hour or two before returning to pick up her young assistant. Polly didn't say much about her conversation with Sam, and Elizabeth had the feeling that it would take more than one meeting before things worked out the way Polly hoped. She seemed cheerful enough, however, when Elizabeth left her at the house.

That afternoon Sadie Buttons arrived in the taxi that Elizabeth had arranged to meet her at the station. Martin opened the door to her, and there followed a few moments of confusion while Sadie tried to explain who she was and why she was there. Alerted by the girl's strident voice, Elizabeth hurried down the stairs to sort things out.

"Madam! This young woman insists she lives here," Martin declared, obviously put out.

"She does, Martin," Elizabeth assured him. "At least, she will from now on. Sadie is our new housemaid." She turned to the beaming girl. "I'm sorry, Sadie. Martin gets confused now and then."

"That's all right, m'm. We all get confused sometimes, don't we, luv?" This last was directed at Martin, and accompanied by a hefty nudge of Sadie's elbow.

Martin drew himself up as best he could. "I *beg* your pardon. Kindly remember to whom you are speaking. I am the butler of this honorable establishment, and as such I demand some respect."

"Oo, hoity-toity, aren't we?" Sadie winked at Elizabeth in a rather vulgar manner. "I'll have to sort him out, I can see that."

"Sort me *out*?" Martin appealed to Elizabeth. "Madam, really! Surely I do not have to tolerate such impertinence in this house?"

"I'll take care of it, Martin. Why don't you run down to the kitchen and let Violet know that Sadie has arrived?"

"Yes, madam." After sending a malevolent glare at the hapless girl, Martin headed for the kitchen stairs at the speed of a disgruntled turtle.

Elizabeth waited until she was sure he was out of earshot before saying quietly, "Don't mind Martin. He's very old and set in his ways, and doesn't understand how things have changed. He thinks this is still the nineteenth century. I must ask that you try to be tolerant, and humor him as best you can."

"Don't you worry, your ladyship. I'll play along. Once he gets used to me, I'll jolly him up a bit."

Elizabeth did her best to hide her apprehension at the thought of Martin being "jollied up." It would seem that Violet would have her hands full with the new maid, after all. Eyeing all the suitcases the girl had brought with her, Elizabeth wondered if the room that Violet had prepared for her would hold everything she'd brought.

Violet chose that moment to appear at the top of the stairs, obviously annoyed at having to attend to the new arrival. "Martin will show you to your room," she said, handing the girl a key. "Once you get settled, come along to the kitchen and we'll go over what needs to be done."

"Okay." Sadie gave her a cheerful grin, then seized a suitcase in each hand. "Better let me carry these down the stairs. The old boy looks as if he'll drop dead from a heart attack at any minute."

"The old boy," Martin said dryly from behind Violet, "is perfectly capable of carrying bags down the stairs." He stepped out into the light. "Follow me, young lady. And please watch your step. I have no wish to break your fall. It would be comparable to having an elephant descend on one."

Elizabeth sent a wary glance at Sadie, and was rewarded with yet another wink. "Proper luv, ain't he? He needs livening up a bit, that's all." She stomped across the hallway and followed Martin down the stairs.

Violet stood staring after them, a worried frown wrinkling her brow. "I'm going to have trouble with those two," she muttered.

Elizabeth smiled. "Look on the bright side, Violet. He'll be so busy defending himself against Sadie's at-

tempts to liven him up, he won't have any sarcasm left
for you."

Saturday morning dawned with clear blue skies and a few
powderpuff clouds dotted here and there. Elizabeth
viewed the sky with mixed feelings. Good weather was
imperative for the success of the fete, but it also meant
that Earl could be sent on a mission and wouldn't be able
to attend.

Nevertheless, she looked forward to the afternoon with
an anticipation she hadn't felt in years. The prospect of
judging the local talent seemed less formidable with the
possibility of sharing the task with Major Earl Monroe.

Even Violet seemed to be in a good mood at breakfast,
no doubt because Sadie was somewhere in the heart of
the manor cleaning bathrooms—a job that Polly had sadly
neglected since she'd been promoted to office assistant.

Polly had done her best to keep up with the jobs that
Violet refused to do, as well as her work in the office. It
would be good for everyone, including Martin, to have an
extra pair of hands in the house. All in all, Elizabeth decided, as she neatly clipped off the top of her soft-boiled
egg, it promised to be a good day.

She was pleasantly surprised later that morning when
Polly arrived at the manor, eager to make up for her lost
days. After making sure the girl seemed well enough to
stay, Elizabeth set her to work with the filing while she
sorted out the various bills that were left to be paid. The
amount still owing depressed her. Fred Bickham's lost
rent would put a hole in the budget.

Frowning, she reached for the letter saying that Fred
was going to Ireland. The last person seen with Fred had
been Reggie Stewart. Was it possible that Reggie had
written the letter? No, he couldn't have done. The letter
had arrived *after* Reggie's body had been discovered. At
least a week after Reggie had died.

No, someone else had sent that letter, hoping that no
one would realize Fred Bickham was missing. Quite pos-

sibly the same person who had beaten Reggie's face to a pulp. She should tell George about it, though it was doubtful anything would be done. As long as Reggie's death had been ruled a heart attack, the inspector was not going to be too concerned about who had beaten him.

No, it was up to her to find out who had written the letter. Glancing at the filing cabinet, where Polly stood sorting through the files, she asked casually, "Do you know what happened to the contents of the wastebasket? I dropped an envelope in there that I need to look at."

"Yes, m'm." Polly turned to look at her. "Sadie came up and emptied it. I expect she put it all in the rubbish bin."

"Thank you, Polly." Elizabeth made a mental note to ask Sadie about the envelope. Still absorbed in the mystery of Fred's disappearance, she tried to remember everything Alfie had told her about that night. As she recalled his words, something he'd said seemed to ring a bell somewhere in her head. She thought about it for a long time before she realized just why Alfie's comments were so significant.

That afternoon, dressed in a rather impractical yellow silk dress and lace-trimmed hat to match, Elizabeth sat in regal splendor on the judge's seat in front of the stage, which had been set up on the lawn in the vicarage gardens.

Dozens of colorful stalls surrounded her, some piled high with knitted hats, gloves, scarves, and socks, while others displayed handmade lace doilies, lace-edged handkerchiefs, and embroidered pillow slips. Dolls and bears made from scraps of fabric shared space with boats, trains, and marvelous little planes carved from broken branches collected in the woods.

There were cakes baked without eggs, and lemonade powder wrapped up in paper cones. The white elephant stall groaned under the weight of old-fashioned costume jewelry and long-forgotten, useless items dragged from dusty cupboards and musty attics and thankfully discarded, only to end up in yet another cupboard or attic in another house until the following year, when the whole procedure would begin again.

The attendance at this year's summer fete appeared to be excellent. Not only were many people from the village present, but Elizabeth spied British soldiers strolling around the vicarage gardens in small groups, as well as several American airmen in the company of young girls.

Hoping fervently that they all remained peaceful, Elizabeth turned her attention to the stage, where Captain Wally Carbunkle was announcing the first contestant. In spite of her best intentions, her mind wandered back to Earl. He hadn't arrived yet and she was plagued with the nagging worry that today might be the day he failed to return from a mission.

There were many other things that could have kept him from joining her that afternoon, she reminded herself. All of them quite uneventful. Even so, the ache behind her rib cage was a distraction, and she had to force her attention on Priscilla Pierce, the earnest, energetic woman seated at the piano.

Priscilla was accompanied by Wilf White, whose wailing harmonica had pained many an ear at the local dances. The third member of the group, a belligerent trumpet player long ago dubbed Awful Ernie by his unappreciative audiences, blasted out his notes and completely overshadowed what Elizabeth assumed was supposed to be a solo piece performed by Priscilla.

Obviously annoyed at this intrusion on her masterpiece, Priscilla was sending dire looks at Ernie, who apparently was completely oblivious to anything except his efforts to belch as much air into the instrument as possible, with complete disregard for tone.

In frustration, Priscilla began pounding the keys while one foot pumped furiously up and down on the sustain pedal of the piano until Elizabeth was quite sure it would fall off. Not to be outdone, Wilf sawed at his mouth with his harmonica, bent almost double with the effort to empty his lungs.

All in all, not a particularly inspiring performance, Elizabeth decided, among a smattering of lukewarm applause. She studied the score sheet, and after much consideration, wrote down a 3, which, considering she had only 10 points to play with, seemed quite generous.

The second volunteer to brave the unforgiving audience turned out to be George Dalrymple, who looked disturbingly unfamiliar without his constable's uniform. After consulting with Priscilla at the piano, he stepped to the center of the stage and laced his hands across his chest.

Priscilla began pounding, and after a second or two, George pursed his lips and blew. Braced for the ear-splitting sound she'd endured in the police station, Elizabeth closed her eyes. Priscilla went on bashing out the notes on the suffering piano, but no sound could be heard from George.

Opening one eye, Elizabeth saw George wipe the back of his hand across his mouth. "Nervous, your ladyship," he called out, as she looked up at him. "Makes me mouth dry."

Elizabeth nodded. "Take your time, George."

By now catcalls from the audience drifted toward the stage. George pursed again, blew again, and managed nothing better than a pitiful little peep. Priscilla stopped playing and sat glaring at poor George, who was becoming quite red in the face. Finally, someone took pity on him and rushed forward with a glass of lemonade.

Instead of wetting George's whistle, so to speak, the tart drink had the opposite effect. George finally had to give up, and left the stage amid much booing and jeering. Wally hurried out to announce the next contestant.

Elizabeth raised her eyebrows when she saw Rita Crumm walk out. Normally Rita occupied the judge's chair, and now Elizabeth realized why she had been handed this exalted position. For the first time since she could remember, Rita Crumm was actually taking part as a contestant.

Filled with expectation, Elizabeth sat back to enjoy the spectacle. Rita was dressed in a uniform that had obviously been homemade, since it bore no resemblance to anything Elizabeth had seen before. Huge gold tassels, apparently confiscated from Rita's front room curtains, swung from her shoulders and dangled across her flat chest. She wore a bus conductor's cap, which had been lavishly trimmed with gold braid.

Priscilla, perched high on her seat, held her hands in a dramatic pose above the piano keys. The audience fell quiet, no doubt as intrigued as Elizabeth to know exactly what talent Rita had so far successfully hidden from the villagers.

Priscilla's hands descended in a deafening crash of discord, making Elizabeth wince. Rita opened her mouth, and in a voice that resembled a stray cat in heat, began belting out the words to a popular song.

Luckily the words were familiar, since the tune was totally unrecognizable. Just when Elizabeth thought she could stand it no more, Rita came to the end of the song. About to politely applaud, Elizabeth's hands froze as the entire Housewives Brigade, consisting of several nervous, fidgety women, marched haphazardly onto the stage and stood in a bedraggled row, valiantly attempting to keep up with their stalwart and very loud leader.

The audience must have been in shock, since not a sound emerged from their open mouths. Struggling to keep a straight face, Elizabeth focused her gaze on Rita as the group of red-faced women battled their way through the final verse.

At last it was over. The song came to an end, Priscilla lifted her hands from the keys, and everyone took a bow—to dead silence. Feeling somewhat responsible for the unfortunate women, Elizabeth clapped vigorously, thus prompting the audience to follow suit, albeit with great reluctance.

Elizabeth stared at the score sheet, agonizing over a suitable score. She failed to see the man take the seat next to her until he said, far too close to her ear, "That had to be the worst rendition of 'We'll Meet Again' I've ever heard."

"That's because it was supposed to be 'The White Cliffs of Dover.' " She smiled at Earl, her relief making her light-headed. "Thank heavens you're here. I'm having the devil of a job deciding on these scores."

His eyes crinkled at the corners. "Is that the only reason you're happy to see me?"

"Of course not." Flustered, she dropped her pencil to the ground. Bending over to pick it up, she bumped heads with Earl, tipping her hat to the back of her head. "Sorry." She hastily straightened her hat, then took the pencil he'd retrieved for her. "Thank you."

Fortunately they were interrupted by the next contestant, a charming little girl who sang a song made famous by Shirley Temple. Enchanted, Elizabeth had no hesitation in declaring her the winner.

Handing her the prize—a crisp one-pound note—amid boisterous cheers from the crowd, Elizabeth breathed a huge sigh of relief. Her duties were over for the afternoon, and for a little while, she could enjoy the scintillating presence of Major Earl Monroe.

CHAPTER

❧ 14 ❧

"Now that I have time to breathe," Elizabeth said, as she strolled around the stalls at Earl's side, "I want to thank you for my St. Christopher medal. That was a very thoughtful gift, and one I shall treasure always."

Earl smiled. "I'm told that St. Christopher is the patron saint of travelers, I thought you could use all the help you can get when you're tearing around on that bike of yours."

She glanced up at him. "Are you suggesting I'm a reckless driver?"

"Not at all. It's the other idiots on the road I worry about." His face sobered. "I gave you the medal to remind you to be careful. Sam's accident makes it seem all the more important now."

"I'll be careful," she promised him. Inside she was glowing to think he worried about her. He had a way of changing the most mundane day into an unforgettable one.

The afternoon turned out to be far more pleasurable

than Elizabeth had anticipated. The sun warmed her back while a light breeze from the ocean cooled her face, and the time passed all too quickly.

Earl proved to be quite proficient at several of the games. Although he had no luck ringing the necks of milk bottles with little hoops, he won a prize at the dartboards, and yet another by rolling coins down a tiny ramp and settling them in the middle of a square.

"I can never do that," Elizabeth said, as she accepted the tiny china elephant he offered her. "My coins always touch the edges of the squares."

"It's all in the wrist." He wriggled his hand at her, making her laugh.

Just then, a worried-looking young man waved a camera at them. "*North Horsham News*, your ladyship. May I take your picture?"

"Of course." Elizabeth smiled up at Earl. "Please excuse me for a moment."

Earl nodded, and stepped away, but the young man waved him back. "No, both of you together, if I may?"

Earl shrugged, and stepped back to her side.

Feeling somewhat self-conscious, Elizabeth smiled at the camera, intensely aware of him standing close beside her.

The reporter thanked them both, then chased off after another prospect. "Well," she said lightly, "that will be a good one for you to send home."

"I'll get a copy?"

"Of course! I always order a copy for the family scrapbook. I'll order one for you, too."

"The family scrapbook?"

"Yes." She led him to a wooden bench set against the wall of the vicarage and sat down. "I need to rest my feet. These heels were not meant for walking on grass."

He sat down beside her, pulled off his cap, and began twisting it around in his hands. "Tell me about the scrapbook."

"Oh, it's nothing spectacular. Just photographs of the family taken over the years."

"I'd like to see it."

Pleased, she said quickly, "I'll show it to you when you have some time to spare."

"I'd like that."

"They are rather fun to look at. It's good to keep a record, don't you think?"

"Absolutely. Especially of a family as illustrious as yours."

She wrinkled her nose. "I must admit, it's a lot simpler now that we have cameras to take the pictures. In the old days one had to have portraits painted." She looked up at him. "Have you noticed that in the portraits of my ancestors in the great hall, not one of them is smiling? They all have these terrible dour expressions on their faces. I made up my mind that when I have my portrait painted, I'm going to smile."

"You're gonna have your portrait painted?"

He sounded amused, and she felt a little defensive. "Well, it is tradition, after all. Though I suppose it all seems rather ostentatious to you."

"Not at all. I think it's great that you want to hang on the wall with the rest of your ancestors. Something to treasure for the rest of your life. As much as I'll treasure the picture we had taken today."

Instantly appeased, she smiled. "As will I. Some of my photographs are more important to me than a treasure chest of jewels. I can look at them and be instantly transported to the moment they were taken. Especially the ones I had taken with my parents. Now that they're gone, the photographs are all I have left to remind me of them."

"I know what you mean. Just about every guy I know carries a picture of someone he loves everywhere he goes. Amazing how important a scrap of paper can be to someone."

She wondered if he carried a photograph of his wife and daughters with him everywhere he went. If so, she really didn't want to see it. Knowing what his family looked like would only make them more real, and the guilt that already kept her awake at night would become even more insistent.

She thought about his last words. She already knew how important the picture taken that afternoon would become to her. Something to keep and treasure in the dark future when the war was over and he was back in his country, where he belonged. Thinking about it made her depressed.

All this talk of photographs reminded her of the blank space on Betty Stewart's wall. Not that Betty had seemed that upset by its loss. Then again, the picture had meant far more to her husband. Reggie Stewart had been so proud of it, according to Joan Plumstone. It was sad to think it had been stolen. Reggie would be devastated if he knew.

Elizabeth frowned. An idea was forming in her head. An idea so bizarre she couldn't believe she was considering it. Yet if she was right, everything she'd discovered up to now would make perfect sense.

When Earl spoke again, she jumped. "Penny for them?"

"Oh, it's nothing. Just something I need to look into." *Something,* she silently added, *that might just tell me what had happened to Fred Bickham the night he left the Tudor Arms in the company of Reggie Stewart.*

Much to her delight, Earl suggested she show him the scrapbook that evening, over a glass of the excellent brandy he brought with him. Sharing her precious memories with him was both exquisite and painful, and by the time he left, she was warding off depression once more.

She tried to overcome it by concentrating on her revelation earlier, and what it might mean in connection with all the other facts she had. Finally she scribbled everything in a notebook, and studied every angle until she was fairly certain her theories were correct.

The next step was to decide what to do about it. Reggie's funeral was to be held the day after tomorrow. She would have to talk to George in the morning, after church.

Having made that decision, she managed to rest easier and slept relatively well that night.

Immediately after the service at St. Matthew's ended, Elizabeth mounted her motorcycle and rode down to George's house. He and Millie hadn't attended church that morning, and she was concerned that one of them might be ill. When she received no answer at the house, she drove by the police station. As she'd expected, the building was locked up tight.

Her next stop was at George's partner's house. Sid Goffin wasn't at home either, but Ethel, his wife, informed Elizabeth that both men were in North Horsham for a bowls tournament. They weren't expected back until late that night.

There was nothing for it, Elizabeth decided. She would have to wait until the morning. She was reluctant to make too big a fuss, in case her theories turned out to be wrong. Most of them were based on conjecture, and she had no concrete proof of anything. Just a solid line of thinking that made perfect sense to her, though whether or not George would share her opinion was in some doubt.

Restless for the rest of the day, and plagued by doubts that night, she was thankful for what little sleep she could manage. She awoke Monday morning in a turmoil of indecision.

Her suspicions would cause a terrible disruption of a sacred and deeply emotional event. If she were mistaken, the consequences would be more than embarrassing. They would be downright humiliating. No one would ever forget what she'd done. She would lose all the respect and admiration she'd worked so hard to earn since her parents' death. It would be a tremendous gamble, yet how else could she prove what she knew deep down had to be true?

Tormented by her tumultuous indecision, she arrived at St. Matthew's for the funeral feeling as if she hadn't slept in a week. The service was mercifully brief, since the vicar seemed to be having trouble finding good things to say about the dead man.

Elizabeth had hoped to find George or Sid at the funeral, but neither of them was there. No doubt their late night had taken its toll and they were using duty as an excuse not to attend.

As everyone filed out of the church, Elizabeth felt quite desperate. If she was going to speak up, it would have to be now. Once the body was buried, it would be much more difficult to persuade people to listen to her wild accusations.

The vicar was talking earnestly to Betty Stewart when he emerged from the church, and Elizabeth couldn't bring herself to approach them. Instead, she sought out the funeral director, Joshua Metcalf, a solemn-looking man with a nervous habit of twitching his nose.

"Such a sad day," he commented, after greeting her. "I've attended hundreds of funerals, but they never cease to depress me. I suppose it's because they are a reminder of how vulnerable we all are, and how very short our time on this earth can be."

"Indeed," Elizabeth agreed. "I didn't know Mr. Stewart that well, but it's never easy to see someone buried in the ground."

"Twice, in this case." Joshua blinked at her, his long, thin nose twitching in unison. "That must have been such a shock for you, Lady Elizabeth, to find the poor man buried in your Victory Gardens. Such a dreadful shock."

"It certainly was." Elizabeth hesitated. "Did you know Mr. Stewart well?"

Joshua shrugged. "As well as one knows the man who delivers the coal, I suppose. I've talked to him several times. Bit of a surly bloke, actually." His nose twitched even more rapidly. "Not that I want to speak ill of the dead, of course."

"Did you . . . happen to notice anything different about him? When you laid him out, I mean."

Joshua's eyebrows arched. "Different? Can't say that I did. Not that I'd notice, of course. Couldn't recognize his face at all. Nasty business, that. What are the constables doing about it, anyway? Have they found out who did that to him?"

"Not yet, as far as I know." Elizabeth glanced over his shoulder to where the vicar was standing by the coffin. It was too late. She couldn't disrupt a funeral without being absolutely certain of her facts. She would simply have to wait until she could talk to George, and hope she could convince him to open a further investigation.

She was about to turn away when Joshua muttered, "I have to say, though, it's the first time I saw the man's nails clean."

Elizabeth paused. "I beg your pardon?"

"Stewart's nails. They were usually caked with coal dust. I haven't seen them that clean since I met the man."

Without bothering to answer him, Elizabeth spun on her heel and headed for the grave site. She had almost reached it when she noticed a man standing in the shadows of a huge oak tree.

His shoulders were hunched, and his checkered cap was pulled low over his eyes. Although the morning mist had dissipated, his tattered raincoat was buttoned to his throat.

Elizabeth instantly recognized both the coat and the cap. She stopped short, staring at the man. He must have caught sight of her, for he turned and limped across the grass, disappearing around the back of the church. There was no doubt about it. The cap, the coat, and the limp all belonged to the missing man—Fred Bickham.

For a second or two she contemplated telling Joshua what she'd seen. If she did that, she realized, her quarry would have disappeared before Joshua had time to do anything about it. She was left with no choice.

She set off after the man, taking care to remain out of sight as she rounded the corner of the ancient stone wall. She was just in time to see him disappear through the rear gate. Tempted to go back for her motorcycle, she aban-

doned the idea. It would take too long, and she might lose
sight of him before she could get the thing started and
into the lane that ran past the back of the church. She
would have to follow on foot, and pray that the man didn't
have a bicycle waiting for him in the lane.

Peeking out past the hedges that bordered the church-
yard, she saw the hunched figure moving rapidly up the
lane. Apparently he intended to cross the fields, giving
him a short cut to the village. Elizabeth waited until he'd
climbed over a gate and dropped to the other side before
moving cautiously forward.

It was easy to follow him through the cornfield. An
uneven pathway of crushed stalks led her across the field
to the fences on the other side. Here the trail ended, but
she was just in time to see the man walking at a brisk
pace down the lane toward the crossroad.

She bent over as she followed him, hiding behind the
hedges and peeking out every now and then to make sure
he was still ahead of her. She had a bad moment when
she reached the crossroad and had to dart forward in full
view, but fortunately the man kept his gaze straight ahead,
and once more she reached the shelter of the thick hedges.

A few minutes later, she wasn't really surprised to see
him turn in at the row of cottages. Where else would the
man go but home?

She waited at the corner until she saw him disappear
up the garden path, then she carefully crept forward. The
front door closed just as she reached the gate.

Realizing that he was probably in the house when she
visited it earlier, she wondered where he had hidden himself. She'd searched the house pretty thoroughly the last
time she was there. Every room, every cupboard, every
closet . . . except the space under the stairs. It was the
place most people planned on using as a shelter in the
event of an air raid. A small, cramped space under the
stairs. But certainly big enough to house a man quite com-
fortably.

She shivered, and glanced at the cottage next door. Perhaps she should wait for Wally Carbunkle to come home. She'd seen him at the funeral. But Wally usually went down to the Tudor Arms for his midday pint. It could be some time before he returned home.

There were no men living in the other cottages, and any of the women who weren't working were probably doing their daily shopping in the High Street. In any case, she could hardly raise the alarm until she had satisfied herself that what she strongly suspected was indeed true.

Having made her decision, she walked boldly up to the cottage and onto the porch. She still carried the key in her handbag, and after fishing it out, she fitted it in the lock and turned it.

She hadn't realized until that moment that the blackout curtains at the windows had been drawn again. She left the door wide open and stepped into the shadowy room, her heart thumping in anticipation.

She stood just inside the doorway, waiting until her eyes adjusted to the shadows. Not a sound emerged from inside the house. Not a creak or a groan from the aging floorboards. Not a whisper or a sigh from a movement anywhere.

She raised her chin, and in a voice that shook only slightly, called out, "Hello? Fred? Fred Bickham! I know you're in here. I'd like to talk to you for a minute. There's a little matter of some overdue rent we have to discuss."

She waited, while the silence seemed to thicken around her.

After a long moment, she approached the kitchen and slowly pushed open the door. The smell was appalling— reminding her of sour milk and rotten eggs. After making sure the room was empty, Elizabeth backed out of there and closed the door.

The hallway was also empty, the door to the space under the stairs firmly closed. She stared at it for a long moment, then moved past it, her skin tingling, to the bottom of the stairs.

The upstairs landing was in darkness. The blackout curtains had to be drawn up there as well. The very last thing she wanted to do was climb those stairs and face those dark, menacing rooms. Once more she called out, her voice echoing up to the ceiling. "Fred? I know you're home. I've come for my rent."

The silence, ominous and threatening, chilled her to the bone. Nevertheless, she forced her feet to move, one step at a time, up and up, until at last she stood on the landing. Again she paused, ears straining for the slightest sound.

When it came, she almost jumped out of her stockings. A sharp creak, from the other side of the bedroom door. She moved forward and rapped on the door with her knuckles. "Fred? Are you in there? Open this door at once."

Again silence greeted her. Grasping the handle, she sent up a silent prayer, then twisted it, pushing the door open. She could see nothing inside the room. Nor could she hear anything. Not even the sound of breathing.

Her instincts told her the room was empty, but it took all her courage to edge around the bed and fling open the heavy black curtains. Spinning around, she let out her breath in an explosive sigh of relief as light flooded the room. She was alone. The creak must have been a contraction of the floorboards.

A quick glance under the bed and a hasty peek into the wardrobe confirmed her conclusion. A brief inspection of the spare bedroom also revealed no occupant. If he was still in the house, he had to be in the only place left . . . under the stairs.

She ran lightly down to the hallway, and stood in front of the little door. "I know you're in there," she said loudly. "So you might as well come out." She rattled the handle, but the door was locked from the inside. It didn't budge. "I can have P.C. Dalrymple break this door down." She pounded on the wood panels. "I'm quite sure he'll be happy to oblige."

She froze as a muffled voice answered her from inside

the tiny space. "If you know what's good for you, you'll get out now."

"I'm not going away," she said firmly. "I know the truth now. I know what happened. And I'm not the only one. Sooner or later they'll find you, so you might as well give up now."

Although she'd been prepared for it, she jumped backward when the door swung open so sharply it almost hit her.

He still wore the cap pulled low on his forehead, and she couldn't see his face clearly at first. But then he lifted his chin, and she caught her breath. She'd been right, after all. It wasn't Reggie Stewart who had been buried at St. Matthew's church that morning. For the simple reason that, at that very moment, she was staring at him.

His voice, when he spoke, was low and menacing. "I might have known you couldn't leave well enough alone. It's just too bad, your bloody ladyship, that you couldn't be sensible and mind your own business. 'Cause now I'll have to do something I really didn't want to do."

Staring into his eyes, Elizabeth realized she'd underestimated him. It was a mistake she'd made once before. And this time, Earl Monroe wasn't around to help her.

CHAPTER
❊ 15 ❊

Sadie Buttons stood in the middle of the great hall and
stared in awe. Violet had ordered her to dust the suit of
armor and put a spot of oil in the hinges. She eyed the
impressive figure with some misgivings. She'd never
dusted a suit of armor before. Didn't seem decent, somehow.

She shook out her duster and advanced on her victim.
"You must have been a big bloke when you was alive,"
she commented. "Wouldn't mind a knight in shining armor meself. Make a change from the bloody twits I usually bump into, I'm telling you."

Speaking out loud made her more comfortable. The silence bothered her a lot. She hadn't said anything to Violet, and she wouldn't dream of mentioning it to Lady
Elizabeth, but the truth was, the Manor House gave her
the willies.

She wasn't quite sure why. Maybe it was because it

was so old, and so flipping huge. Maybe it was the shadows that seemed to move about, or that creepy old geezer, Martin, what with him muttering to himself and shuffling around like his feet was tied together.

"You'd protect me, though, wouldn't you, luv?" She leaned back into the crook of the armor's bent arm and gazed up at the empty helmet. "Oh, my, how strong you are. I could have done with you in the Blitz." She flapped her hand back and forth with an imaginary fan. "Quite take my breath away, you do."

Reaching into her bucket, she pulled out a small bottle of machine oil. "You'll have to excuse me, sire, for messing about with your helmet." She lifted the visor. "Violet wanted me to put a spot of oil in here for you. Make your choppers work better, it will."

After squeezing a drop into each corner of the visor, she studied her handiwork. "Wonder how you ate through that thing? Must have spilled a lot of beer down your shirt, that's what I think."

The visor clacked back in place, and at the same time, a soft whisper of sound echoed down the massive hall. Sadie jumped back, and peered into the gloomy shadows. She could have sworn she'd heard someone giggle. Sounded like a child, it did.

Staring at the empty walls, she shook her head. "Must be imagining things," she said, turning back to the armor. "There ain't no children in the Manor House. Though, if you ask me, the place would be a lot brighter if there was."

She flicked the duster across the broad shoulders. " 'Course, this place probably looks nice and modern to you. I mean, you must have lived in them drafty castles when you was fighting in the wars."

She reached behind to dust the armor's back. "Must be lonely, standing here all the time, with no one to talk to. See the Yanks, much, do you? Probably not. They have their own way out down the back stairs. They wouldn't come along here anyway."

She moved around in front of the metal figure again and began dusting its belly. "I ain't seen much of them neither. Not sure I want to, after all the gossip in the village about them. Except for the major, of course. Good-looking bloke, that major. Might fancy spending an hour or two with him in the back row of the flicks."

Her hand froze as a soft giggle drifted clearly down the hall. She hadn't imagined it, after all. What she'd heard was very definitely a child giggling. But if there was a child in the great hall, she couldn't see it.

She crouched down, her duster vigorously polishing the knee plates. Without raising her head, she peered side-ways down the hall. She wasn't quite sure if she was imagining things or not, but she could swear she saw the heavy gold curtains at the windows move ever so slightly.

She straightened her knees and gave the knight a final flick with her duster. "There you are, me old cock spar-rer—good as new. Don't say I don't look after you. Maybe one day you can come to me rescue, and ride off with me on your white horse. You'd have to get rid of that armor, though. Bit rough on me tender spots, that'd be."

Pursing her lips, she started whistling as she walked down the hall toward the east wing. The bucket in her hand swung to and fro, and she gazed up at each of the massive portraits as she drew closer and closer to the enormous square-paned windows.

She was almost even with the curtains now, and without turning her head, she glanced sideways at them. Peeking out just below the bottom of one of them was the toe of a very small shoe.

Sadie Buttons might not look very agile, but she could move at the speed of lightning when she wanted to. Letting go of the bucket, she made a dive at the curtains. "Gotcha!" she yelled, as her arms closed around a small, wriggling body. A shriek loud enough to deafen her rang in her ears.

It took her a moment or two to disentangle the body

from the suffocating curtains, but finally she dragged the small child from the dusty folds. The little face was streaked with dirt and her golden hair was a mass of tangles. She wore a red dress covered in stains, and her hands were filthy.

Holding a skinny arm firmly in her grasp, Sadie glared at the child and fiercely demanded, "Just what the bloomin' blazes do you think you're doing?"

The little girl opened her mouth and bawled. At the same time Sadie felt a thump in the middle of her back. Startled, she spun around, almost losing her grip on the child. To her astonishment, two more children stood glaring up at her.

Both girls looked as grimy as the one Sadie had captured, and the oldest, who couldn't have been more than eleven, stood with her fists clenched, her brown eyes glowering with hostility. " 'Ere," she snarled, raising her small fists, "you let 'er go or I'll sock you in the jaw."

"You'd have to reach it first," Sadie said grimly. "Who are you, and where did you come from?"

"None o' your bleeding business."

"Well, I'm making it my business, so there. If you don't start talking right now, I'm taking this one to the kitchen and I'm ringing the rozzers and they'll come and put her in jail."

The girl went on glaring at her, but the child at her side started whimpering. "Don't let the bobbies take her away, miss. We didn't do nothing wrong. Honest."

Sadie looked the eldest girl in the eye. "If you didn't do nothing wrong, then you can tell me what you're all doing here."

For a moment it seemed there would be a deadlock, but then the child shrugged her bony shoulders. "We was evacuated, wasn't we?"

"Evacuated? From where?"

"From London, silly. Where else?"

Sadie shook her head in bewilderment. "You was sent to the Manor House? Why didn't no one tell me?"

" 'Coz we wasn't sent here and no one knows we're here, that's why."

Sadie took a deep breath. "What are your names?"

"I'm Patsy." The child jerked a thumb at the little girl by her side. "She's Maureen and that's Jenny."

Sadie looked down at the tot she was holding, whose sobs had finally quieted to loud sniffs. "Well, I'm Sadie. You look as if you could use a glass of milk, Jenny. Wanta come with me to the kitchen?"

Jenny flicked a glance at Patsy, then nodded.

"I think you all better come with me." Sadie started walking down the hall, her bucket in one hand and the child tightly gripped with the other. Jenny trotted obediently at her side. Looking over her shoulder, Sadie was satisfied to see the other two trailing behind her at a distance.

The little group descended the stairs while Sadie chatted about anything that came into her head to keep the girls' attention as they approached the kitchen door. Nudging it open with her foot, Sadie prayed that Violet would be in there.

The housekeeper stood at the sink, washing potatoes under the tap. She spoke without turning around. "Finished already? That was quick. I hope you did a good job of cleaning those lavatories—"

"I brought some visitors."

"Visitors?" Violet spun around, a fat potato in one hand. "Who—?" Her jaw dropped, and she stared at the three children as if they had floated down from the moon.

"I found them in the great hall, hiding behind the curtains." Sadie beckoned to each one. "That's Patsy, that's Maureen, and this is Jenny. They was evacuated from London."

Violet dropped the potato in the sink. "Then what in the world are they doing here?"

Patsy appeared ready for a fight. "We ran away, that's wot."

Violet stared at her. "Ran away? From who?"

"From the people we was sent to. They was cruel and mean, and they kept hitting us." She grabbed Maureen by the shoulders, spun her around and began unbuttoning her cotton dress.

Sadie and Violet stared speechless at the ugly purple bruises on the child's back. "That's what they did to her," Patsy said, her voice trembling for the first time. "All because she forgot to say please."

"Oh, my good Gawd," Sadie whispered.

Violet cleared her throat, and appeared to have trouble speaking for a moment. "Come and sit down here," she said at last. "I'll get you all something to drink. Lunch is almost ready, you can have it with us. Then you can tell us all about it." She glanced at Sadie. "You get back up there and finish your jobs. I'll take care of them. Though what her ladyship is going to say when she sees them, heaven only knows." She glanced at the clock. "You haven't seen her, have you, Sadie? The funeral was over at least an hour ago. She told me she was coming straight back here. It's not like her to be late for a meal."

Sadie shook her head. "Haven't seen no sign of her." She nodded her head at the children. "You going to be all right with them?"

Violet smiled. "Don't worry, I know how to take care of children. At least I know now who's been stealing food from the larder."

"We didn't take all that much," Patsy said, sounding less hostile now that things appeared to be working out all right.

Sadie left the kitchen, murder in her heart for the monsters who would hurt little tots like that. Deserved to be hung, drawn, and quartered, they did. Just wait until Lady Elizabeth found out. She was the kind of person who would make the rotters pay for what they done. She wouldn't let no one get the better of her. Not her. She knew how to take care of things, Lady Elizabeth did. Comforted by the thought, Sadie tramped back to the bathrooms.

• • •

There were times when words failed Elizabeth, and this was definitely one of them. She stared helplessly at the man emerging from under the stairs, knowing that trying to run for it was futile. He'd be on her before she could reach the front door. Her best hope was to talk her way out of this nasty situation, but right then she couldn't seem to think straight.

"Like I said, your ladyship, you really shouldn't go around poking your nose into things that don't concern you." Reggie pulled the cap from his head and ran his hand through his thinning hair. "Too bad, that. I was hoping you wouldn't twig it until after I got away."

"I assume your wife buried Fred Bickham this morning," Elizabeth said, finding her voice at last.

Reggie's smile was totally without humor. "She's lucky she didn't get buried with him. She's the one what caused all this in the first place. Carrying on with that bank bloke. Good luck to him, that's what I say. If he can stand her nagging, he's a better man than I am, that's for sure."

"Why did you kill Fred?"

She'd hoped to catch Reggie off guard, and apparently she succeeded. His head jerked up. " 'Ere, I didn't bloody kill no one. I spent the night with Bickham here, and when I woke up in the morning, he was dead. We'd been drinking down at the pub the night before. I reckon the beer got to him. He had a bad heart, so he told me."

Elizabeth edged out of the hallway into the living room, her heart leaping in apprehension as he followed her much too closely. "He died after or before you beat up his face?"

His smile faded. "I told you, he was already bloody dead when I woke up."

"Then why did you beat him? Why did you bury him? Why didn't you just tell the police he'd died in bed?"

" 'Cos I thought they might not believe me. At least, that's why I didn't go to them at first."

Elizabeth took another step backward. "And then?"

Reggie's face turned belligerent. "I don't have to answer none of your questions, so just shut up a minute while I work out what I'm going to do with you."

"If Fred died before you beat him," Elizabeth said quietly, "then you didn't kill him. You have nothing to worry about. I don't think there's a penalty for beating someone who's already dead. If you hurt me in any way, however, you will be guilty, and the police will hunt you down. So it would be in your best interests to let me go unharmed."

Reggie scowled. "How the hell do you know what's in my best interests? You don't know all of it, do you? How could you bloody know?"

He stepped forward, forcing Elizabeth backward. The seat of the armchair caught her behind the knees, and she sat down abruptly. "Why don't you tell me all of it?" she said faintly. "Then perhaps I can understand, and find a way to help you."

"Nothing's gonna help me now." Reggie moved between her and the front door, effectively barring her way. "But if you must know, Lady Big Nose, I'll tell you. I had a row with the missus, didn't I? I'd had enough of her hanky-panky, and I couldn't stand her nagging and whining anymore. So I went and joined the Army just to get away from her."

Reggie passed a hand across his eyes. "Stupid. Bleeding stupid, I was. When I got down to the pub that night, Fred was talking about all the 'orrible things that happened to soldiers on a battlefield. I got sick just thinking about it. I knew I'd made a mistake, but I didn't know what to do about it. I didn't want to go home, back to that lying, mouthy tart, so when Fred said I could stay here for a bit, I jumped at it. I thought it would give me time to decide what to do." Reggie started pacing back and forth, obviously agitated.

"And then Fred died," Elizabeth prompted.

"Yeah, he must have died in his sleep. The more I thought about it, the more sense it made. We looked a lot alike. Same height and weight, more or less. So I smashed his face in so no one would recognize him, changed clothes with him, and buried him in John Rickett's garden. I knew John wasn't going to be doing any digging there. By the time anyone found Fred, I reckoned, they'd all think he was me. And I'd be free. No more nagging, lying, cheating wife, and no bloody Army. I could go anywhere and be anyone I wanted. Start all over again, like."

"So why did you wait so long? Why didn't you just leave?"

Reggie shrugged. "Well, if I was going to really be free, I needed money, didn't I?"

"Is that why you stole the picture frame?"

He stared at her. "How did you know about that?"

Elizabeth shifted her weight to the edge of the chair. "Betty told me the house had been robbed and the photograph had been taken. I couldn't understand why the thief didn't take the candlesticks as well. But all you wanted was food and clothes, and what little cash was lying around. You didn't take the frame for its value, you took what it held. The photograph that meant so much to you."

"Very clever, your ladyship. Bleeding brilliant, you are."

"I still don't understand why you didn't leave."

"I told you, I needed money."

Elizabeth stared at him. "Of course. Betty knew, didn't she? She knew it wasn't you she was burying."

"Too right she knew. But she wasn't going to say nothing, was she? She's been wanting that Henry bloke from the bank for weeks. He wouldn't have nothing to do with her while she was married, so it suited her really nice when they dug up my dead body. I was hoping she had a bit stashed away in her drawer, but it wasn't enough to get me farther than North Horsham. So I went back the next night. That's when we made a bargain. She'd get the bit of savings we had out of the bank and give it to me, and I'd disappear forever. She could have Henry and I'd have my freedom."

"Couldn't you have just divorced?"

Reggie snorted. "We're bleeding Catholic, aren't we? Catholics can't get divorced. Besides, who was going to believe me when I told them Fred was dead, after I bashed in his face? No one, that's who. Them stupid constables would have locked me up, and I'd be had up for murder."

"Well, I do believe you didn't kill Fred." Elizabeth put her hands on the arms of the chair. "And if I do, others will, too. You'll never really be free, Reggie, unless you admit to the police what you did, and take the consequences."

"There's not a bloody chance in hell of me doing that. Even if I got off for murder, I'd either end up with a nagging wife I can't stand, or I'd be stuck in the trenches fighting for me life. So just forget it and stop nagging. You're getting as bad as my bleeding wife, and that's the truth."

He started pacing again, taking a longer path each time. Elizabeth eyed the space between her and the door. Maybe, if she made a dash for it just as he was turning, she could make it to the door.

Perhaps Wally Carbunkle would be home by now, or one of the housewives. Surely someone would hear her and send up an alarm. She eased forward, her weight on the balls of her feet. It would have to be the precise moment he turned, so that he'd be off balance.

"It was the watch, wasn't it?" she said, as he passed in front of her. "That's how Betty knew it wasn't you. She took the watch George Dalrymple gave her, but she knew it wasn't yours. You didn't wear a watch. You asked Alfie the time when you left the pub that night. It was Fred's watch. The one thing you forgot to change."

"Yeah, well, I wasn't exactly thinking straight. I couldn't think of everything."

"And it was you who wrote the note saying Fred was going to Ireland."

"He told me he always wanted to go to Ireland." Reggie

flashed her a sinister smile. "I thought it was a nice touch."

"Except that Fred doesn't have a brother in Ireland. Alfie told me his only family was a sister in Devon."

To her dismay, he halted and came to stand in front of her. "Got it all worked out, didn't you? Why didn't you say something if you knew so much?"

"Because I wasn't sure. I knew someone had been in the cottage since the night Fred disappeared. The pillows and bedclothes had been straightened since the first time I came here. I thought at first it was Fred, but then things started falling into place. The black dust on the stair rail was coal dust. Once you get it into your clothes it's almost impossible to get out."

"Too right. Which is why I'm wearing Fred's clothes now. Nice that we're the same size, isn't it? I'm surprised you recognized me at the funeral. I even tried to limp like him."

"I just wasn't sure. I had to be sure if I was going to disrupt a funeral. If I'd been wrong, it would have been most distressing for everyone." Hoping to send him pacing again, she looked up at him. "Why did you go to the funeral?"

"Betty was supposed to give me the money there. I didn't want to risk going to the house again. That nosy neighbor of ours knows everything that goes on." He started pacing again. "Besides, I thought I should be at my own funeral. I suppose I was curious to see if anyone would come and see me buried. I thought if anyone saw me, they'd just think it was Fred. But then you had to go and mess everything up, didn't you? I knew as soon as I saw you coming toward me, there was going to be trouble."

He reached the edge of the room and began to turn. Seizing her chance, Elizabeth propelled herself from the chair and hurtled across the room. She barely managed to crack the door before Reggie pounced on her from behind. Her frantic scream was cut off by his hand across her mouth, and his voice whispered words that filled her with dread.

"Oh, no, your ladyship. You're not going anywhere. I can't let anyone else know I'm still alive. You're going to have a nice rest under the stairs. I'll have to tie you up, I'm afraid, so you can't get out. By the time they find you, it will be too late. The next funeral at St. Matthew's Church will be for the sad passing of the lady of the manor. God rest her bloomin' soul."

CHAPTER

❈ 16 ❈

Violet eyed the solemn faces of the three children. "All right, if you want something to eat, you'll have to earn it. Patsy, you can pull up three extra chairs from over there." She nodded at the far wall. "Maureen, you can help me lay the table." She squatted down in front of the smallest child. "Let's see, Jenny, what can you do to earn your supper?"

Jenny's face screwed up as if she were about to cry. "I've got to wait 'til supper?"

Violet smiled. "No, dearie, I was joking. You'll have lunch with the rest of us. I've got a nice stew on the stove, and tapioca pudding for afters."

Jenny's little face brightened. "I like tabi . . . that white stuff."

"Well, that's settled then." Violet straightened. "You can lay out the serviettes. One next to each plate. We won't have much elbow room, but we'll manage."

Patsy dragged a kitchen chair to the table. "Will Sadie have lunch with us?"

"Sadie usually has hers later, after she's finished her jobs." Violet handed Jenny a pile of white linen serviettes. "But Martin will be here any minute, and Polly will be down from the office, and I expect Lady Elizabeth will be here, too."

"Is that the pretty lady what lives here?" Maureen asked.

Violet gave her a sharp look. "Just how long have you three been hiding in the Manor House?"

Maureen shrugged, and Patsy said quickly, "Only a few days, honest. We didn't have nowhere else to go."

"How did you get here?"

"On a hay cart. Farmer Jenkins was taking a load of wheat to the market, and we hid in it. When he stopped at the crossroad, we got off. That's when we saw this big house on the hill. I thought it was such a big house, no one would notice if we hid in it. And no one would have"—she glared at Jenny—"if someone hadn't made a noise after I told them not to."

Jenny responded by sticking out her tongue.

"Well," Violet said briskly, "I suppose we'll have to notify this Farmer Jenkins that you've been found. They must be worried about you. Not to mention your parents. They must be worried to death."

"Please don't send us back." Maureen started to cry. "I don't want to go back to that nasty, mean man. I want to go home. I want me mum."

"So do I!" Jenny started crying, too, and even Patsy's lower lip began to tremble.

"All right, all right, no one's going to send you back there, don't you worry." Violet glanced at the clock. "When Lady Elizabeth gets home, we'll all sit down and discuss it. She'll know what to do."

"She won't send us back, will she?" Patsy asked anxiously.

"Not when she knows what those bug . . . beggars did to you. Now let's get this table laid, so we can sit down the minute she gets here."

Violet looked up as the door swung open to reveal Martin, one hand still raised, his face a mask of astonishment as he stared at the children.

After a long moment, he found his voice. "I say, I say, I say! What do we have here?"

Jenny giggled nervously, and her sisters stared at the butler with wary eyes.

"We have three guests, Martin. This is Miss Patsy, Miss Maureen, and Miss Jenny."

Martin looked solemnly from one to the other. "How do you do? I'm very pleased to make your acquaintance."

The girls mumbled a reply.

Martin looked at Violet. "I don't think the master would be happy to know his daughters are playing in the kitchen. I remember how testy he was when he discovered Lady Elizabeth here."

Violet sighed. "These are not the master's daughters, Martin. The master had only one daughter. These three are simply our guests."

"Oh, no." Martin shuffled forward, and all three girls retreated behind Violet. "I recognize them. I've seen them talking to the master in the great hall many times."

Violet gave up. "Very well, Martin. The girls will be joining us for lunch. Please see that they are seated." She glanced one last time at the clock. "It doesn't look as if her ladyship intends to join us today."

Martin grasped the back of a chair and hauled on it in an attempt to pull it out from the table. The chair didn't budge.

After watching his second attempt, Patsy boldly went up to him, took hold of the slats in the back of the chair, and lifted it out.

"Oh, I say, jolly decent of you, Miss."

Martin reached for the second chair, but Patsy darted ahead of him and pulled out all the chairs from the table.

"My grandad's old like you," she told him. "We have to help him lift things, too."

"Old?" Martin did his best to straighten his back. "I can assure you, young lady, I am not old."

"No, he was born with wrinkles and those five gray hairs," Violet muttered.

Maureen giggled.

Just then the door swung open again. Expecting to see Elizabeth standing there, Violet opened her mouth to ask why she was late, then closed it again when she saw Major Monroe frowning at her.

"Excuse the intrusion," he said sharply, "but have you seen Elizabeth?"

Violet lifted her chin. "*Lady* Elizabeth is not here at present. If you'd care to leave a message—"

She broke off as the major advanced into the room. His gaze flicked over the curious faces of the children, then fastened on her face. "*Lady* Elizabeth," he said deliberately, "went to a funeral this morning. Her motorbike is parked outside the church. The funeral was over two hours ago. The lady is not at the church, and no one seems to know where she is."

"No doubt her ladyship is visiting one of her tenants."

"Without taking her motorbike?"

"That does sound a bit odd." Violet frowned. "You don't think—"

"I don't know what to think." Earl flicked another glance at the children. "Though I do think we should discuss this outside."

Violet bent over the stove to turn down the gas under the stew. "All right, you three, you can start with a slice of bread and marge. I'll be right back to dish out the stew. Talk to Martin until I get back."

As she followed the major out the door, she heard Patsy ask Martin, "Why do you wear such funny clothes?"

Violet could only guess what kind of answer the child would get.

Out in the hallway, she gazed up at the major with a

sinking feeling in the pit of her stomach. "You sound as if you think something's happened to Lady Elizabeth."

"I'm worried, that's all. I just happened to pass by the church, and saw her motorcycle. I stopped to say hi, but she wasn't there. And she's not here. So where did she go without her motorbike?"

The major had a grim expression on his face that made Violet nervous. "It does seem a bit strange she just went off and left it. Not like her at all. And she was supposed to be home for lunch. She usually lets me know if she's going to be late."

"Right. I guess I'd better go look for her." He glanced at his watch. "Any ideas where to start looking?"

Wary of jumping to the wrong conclusions, Violet wasn't sure how to answer him. Lizzie had said nothing to her about where she might be going after the funeral. "Well, I suppose she could be anywhere. She could be at Bessie's tea room, or the town hall. She could be visiting one of her tenants . . . or she could be shopping in the High Street."

"I'll try them all. I've got a couple of hours before I have to be back at the base. In the meantime, if she comes home, tell her to stay put until I get in touch with her. I'll try to call from the village before I go back to the base."

Beginning to feel worried now, Violet nodded. "Let me know if you find her."

Earl touched the brim of his cap with his fingers. "Promise. Don't worry, she's probably fine. You know how sometimes she gets a bee in her bonnet and takes off without thinking. Probably didn't intend to take so long over whatever it was."

She did know, but it intrigued her that the major knew Lizzie well enough to know it, too. One thing he was wrong about, however. She would never just forget about her motorcycle. Something pretty important must have taken her away from that, and kept her away all this time.

Whatever it was, Violet reflected as she returned to the kitchen, she had an uneasy feeling it wasn't good.

Elizabeth winced as Reggie jammed a face flannel in her mouth and bound it with adhesive tape. Already her arms and legs were tingling with the pain of being strapped tightly into the chair. Her jaw ached where he'd hit her with his fist when she wouldn't stop struggling and yelling. She just prayed he wouldn't hit her again.

"I should kill you here and now," Reggie muttered, rubbing his shin where her well-aimed kick had connected with bone. "But that would make it too easy on you. I'll let you suffer here in the dark, until you run out of air, or starve to death. Whatever comes first. Though I do hear that a person dies pretty quick from thirst."

Guessing that it was more a case of his not having the stomach to kill her, Elizabeth sat quietly, afraid of setting off that vicious temper again.

Finally, he was done. He backed out of the cramped space and bent low to peer at her. "Sorry I can't leave a light on for you. I don't want it shining through the cracks. Not that you're going to need a light for long. Farewell, your ladyship. I'll think of you when I'm sailing for Ireland."

The door closed, and she was plunged into darkness.

Immediately, her brain buzzed with questions. How soon would Violet realize she was missing? How long would it be before someone thought to look for her here? Even if someone came to the cottage, would anyone think to look under the stairs? It was doubtful. With the thick flannel in her mouth, she could barely muster a low whimper. No one would hear her through the heavy paneling.

She peered in the direction of the door, looking in vain for light. In spite of Reggie's fears, there didn't seem to be the slightest crack in the thick boards. Unless someone had the sense to think of opening the door, she could be trapped there for days. Weeks. Forever.

A tremendous wave of depression almost overwhelmed

her. She tried to fight it. Tried not to think about what might happen to her. Tried, instead, to look on the positive side. Someone would find her. Someone had to think of searching Fred's empty cottage.

Her pulse leaped as she remembered something. Sadie! She'd given her orders to come down and clean the cottage. Her spirits sank again almost immediately. But not until tomorrow. How could she stand it, sitting here through an endless day and night that merged into endless hours of blackness?

What if she couldn't make Sadie hear her when she did get there? How long before the air in this tiny, stuffy crawl space gave out? Would the girl think to open the door under the stairs? All she could hope was that her new housemaid was that thorough. And until then, she had a long, lonely wait.

"I think we should give all three girls a bath," Violet declared, when Sadie returned to the kitchen late that afternoon. "They'll look a lot more presentable when Lady Elizabeth comes home."

Sadie ushered the three loudly complaining girls out of the kitchen, leaving Violet alone to pace back and forth, agonizing over what to do. She tried to ignore the cold feeling in her stomach that kept getting stronger with each passing hour. The major had rung more than an hour ago to say he hadn't found Elizabeth and had to get back to the base. He'd suggested that Violet ring the police, but she was reluctant to do that. Lizzie would never forgive her if she raised a hue and cry over nothing.

Yet, as the afternoon hours dragged on without any word from her, Violet was beginning to think she might have to do that after all. Polly kept coming down to the kitchen, asking if there was any word, until Violet finally lost patience and ordered her to go home and rest.

Finally, after yet another hour passed without any word, she lifted the telephone and rang the police station.

"It's about Lady Elizabeth," she told George, when he

answered. "I don't know where she is. I think she might be missing."

"That's usually the case when you can't find someone," George said, in his slow, irritating voice.

Violet gritted her teeth. "George, I don't need any of your sarcasm. Lady Elizabeth's motorcycle has been parked outside the church since early this morning. No one has seen her since then. She wouldn't just go off and leave that motorcycle, and she wouldn't miss a meal without letting me know. She's never been gone this long without me knowing where she is."

"There's a first time for everything," George said.

Sid's voice rang out in the background. "Ain't that the truth."

Violet closed her eyes and prayed for patience. "George, I'm telling you, something is wrong. If you don't start looking for her ladyship this minute, I'm ringing headquarters in North Horsham and complaining to the inspector."

"All right, all right, keep your hair on." George sounded irritable now. "Did she say where she was going?"

"Just to the funeral. She was supposed to come home for lunch."

"All right. We'll look. But if she's sitting in someone's parlor supping on tea and biscuits, Sid and I are not going to be too happy. It costs money to use the services of the constables, you know."

"Just find her, George." Violet replaced the receiver, hesitated for a moment, then looked up the number of the American air base. It took a moment or two for her call to go through, but finally Earl's deep voice came on the line.

"Major Monroe here."

"Major, I'm so sorry to bother you." Violet lost her voice for a moment, and pressed her lips together.

"What is it, Violet? Is Elizabeth home?"

For once she didn't correct him for his lack of a proper

title. "No, Major, I'm afraid she isn't. I've rung the constables. They're looking for her."

There was a slight pause, then Earl said sharply, "Look, I'm almost done here. I'll be there as soon as I can."

Briefly closing her eyes, Violet hung up the telephone. There were times when having a man around the house could be quite comforting.

Earl arrived less than an hour later, by which time Violet had fed the girls and helped Sadie make up beds for them in one of the spare bedrooms. Sadie volunteered to read them a story from one of Elizabeth's childhood books, and having settled them for the night, Violet returned to the kitchen.

There she found the major pacing restlessly around the table while Martin sat recounting his experiences when he first arrived at the Manor House more than fifty years ago.

One look at Earl Monroe's face told Violet that he took Elizabeth's disappearance very seriously. "I've talked to the police," he said, as soon as she walked in the room, "and they're conducting a search. I offered to round up my officers and help. Your constable said something about contacting Rita Crumm?"

Violet made a face. "Under the circumstances, I suppose it might be a good idea. Not that her mob are much use at anything, but they'll be extra pairs of eyes."

"Right. Well, I'd better get on it right away."

A sudden vision of Lizzie lying hurt and alone somewhere froze Violet's blood. "I'll come, too. I can't just sit around here worrying about her."

"Where are we going?" Martin demanded. "Is it the invasion? Are we being evacuated? What about the master's daughters? We can't leave them here." He struggled up from his chair. "Where is my blunderbuss? I'll take the blighters' heads off."

"Sit down, Martin," Violet said sharply. "We're not being invaded. We're just looking for someone, that's all."

Earl nodded his head in Martin's direction. "Someone

had better stay here, in case Elizabeth should return home. You'll need to get the word out."

Violet sighed. "I suppose you're right." Earl started to turn away, and she grasped his sleeve. "Please find her, Major. Bring her home to me."

His bleak expression deepened her fears. "I'll do everything in my power to find her and bring her back with me."

She could ask no more than that.

The door closed behind him, leaving her alone with Martin.

"If anyone can find madam, that gentleman will do so," Martin said quietly. "He cares about her."

Startled by his unexpected moment of coherence, Violet muttered, "We all care about her, Martin. If anything's happened to her. . . ."

"Now, now, no point in going on about it." Martin tapped his long, bony fingers on the table. "I have to talk to the master. He'll know what to do."

For once, Violet didn't have the heart to argue with him.

Long into the night, Earl and his men searched for Elizabeth. Disregarding the rules for blackout, they used torches to probe through the bushes and undergrowth in the thick woods at the edge of the manor's grounds. Fanning out, they worked their way over the downs as far as the cliffs, and along the coast road to the village.

George and Sid started going from cottage to cottage, and at each one they were joined by the tenants, until most of the villagers were out in force, all looking for signs of the missing woman. Rita and her band of housewives, armed with kitchen knives and heavy saucepans, searched the High Street and its narrow alleyways.

As the dawn lightened the sky, George finally called a halt to the search and insisted everyone go home. Even Earl had to admit defeat. His officers were needed at the base, and they had lost a night's sleep. He could not keep them from their duties, much as he hated to give up.

When he returned to the house, Violet fed him breakfast and brewed a pot of coffee for him. She sat with him at the kitchen table, sharing a mug of the coffee with him. "You must be exhausted," she said, gazing with concern at the heavy shadows under his eyes.

He nodded. "Tired and defeated. This isn't a big town. I can't think where she could be."

"Maybe someone took her away," Violet said, voicing her worst fears.

Earl looked at her. "Don't even think that."

"I don't want to, but—"

"We'll find her," he said fiercely.

Now that she'd accepted the worst, Violet thought miserably, she might as well say the rest. "What if she found out who buried Reggie Stewart? What if he killed her and buried her?"

Earl groaned and hid his face in his hands. "Don't you think I've thought about that? How many times did I warn her to stay out of that mess? Why couldn't she listen to me?"

Violet struggled hard to keep her voice from breaking. "When it comes to helping out her people," she said unsteadily, "her ladyship won't listen to anyone but herself."

"So I noticed." Earl lifted his head, his eyes redrimmed. "I've got to find her. Somehow, damn it, I've got to find her."

Violet's heart went out to him. He was a good man, after all. "Get some rest, Major." She got up wearily from her chair. "Get some rest, then we'll decide what to do next."

His next words filled her with a cold dread far worse than anything she'd ever felt before.

"The worst of it is," Earl said heavily, "I have this awful feeling that if I don't find her soon, it may be too late."

CHAPTER

❊ 17 ❊

"What's going to happen to our evacuees?" Sadie asked, as she packed tins of cleaners and rags into a large leather shopping bag. "Where are they, anyway?"

"They're in the office with Polly." Violet swished the dishes around in the soapy suds. "We'll have to wait until Lady Elizabeth comes back. She'll decide what to do about them."

"What if she doesn't come back? What if they never find her?"

"They have to find her." Violet smacked a wet bowl onto the draining board. "We just can't manage without her."

"But what if they don't find her? What about the Manor House, then? If she doesn't come back, who will be the next lady of the manor? Her ladyship doesn't have any heirs, does she? Will there be a new earl, or what?"

Violet crashed a handful of spoons on the board so

violently that one of them bounced off and clattered to the floor. "For Gawd's sake, Sadie Buttons, stop talking about her ladyship as if she were dead already. Go and tell Polly to bring those children down here, and then she can get down to the village. They'll need her to help with the search party."

Sadie pouted. "Why can't I go and search with them? Why do I have to clean that old cottage today?"

"Because her ladyship ordered you to, that's why. It was the last order she gave, and when she comes back she'll expect it done. There's enough people out there searching for her. They won't blinking miss you. So get on with it."

"All right, all right, I'm going." Sadie heaved the bag into her arms. "But if she doesn't come back, it'll all be a waste of time, won't it?"

Violet turned on her, her fear fueling her temper. "If I hear you say one more word about her ladyship not coming back, I swear I'll box your ears until your head rings."

Sadie lifted her chin. "It's not my fault she's missing."

"It'll be your fault if I throw this plate at you." Violet lifted her hand.

"Temper, temper!" Sadie smiled sweetly and darted out the door as Violet pulled back her arm.

Muttering to herself, Sadie stomped across the courtyard in search of the bicycle Violet said she could use. Just her luck to land a job like this, only to have the boss disappear. If her ladyship was a goner, she'd probably have to go back to the Smoke. Or maybe she could get a job at the local boozer. She'd do all right pulling pints for the Yanks. Be more fun than cleaning bathrooms. 'Course, she'd have to find somewhere else to live. And she wouldn't get free meals. She'd have to pay for gas and electricity. And she liked having the Manor House as her address, even if it was big and creepy. So her ladyship had better come home.

Spotting the rusty bicycle leaning against one of the stalls in the stables, Sadie wheeled it out into the warm sun. It had been a while since she rode a bicycle, and with the heavy bag swinging from the handlebars, it took her a few moments to get her balance. Finally she felt secure enough to start down the driveway, and managed to reach the end of it without falling off.

Her wobbly descent of the hill raised the hairs on the back of her neck, and the brakes weren't working too well when she reached the bottom, but she made it to the cottage in one piece.

The key she'd been given was hard to turn in the lock, but she finally got the door open. Walking into the living room, she wrinkled her nose. The place smelled funny, and she couldn't see a thing with the black curtains drawn at the windows.

She dropped her bag in the middle of the floor and hurried across the room to draw back the thick, dusty curtains. Sunlight flooded the room and, looking around, she groaned out loud. The place was filthy. Thick with dust and grime. It would take her all day to get it clean. Muttering to herself, she got to work.

Elizabeth lifted her head, blinking hard to stay awake. Something had disturbed her fitful sleep. She wasn't sure what it was, but she strained her ears, hoping to hear a sound—any sound that would tell her someone was in the cottage and would get her out of this awful blackness.

When the sound she was waiting for finally came, her heart leaped with hope. Above her head she heard the stairs creak, one at a time. Someone was in the house! It had to be Sadie.

Elizabeth took a deep breath. Her throat was so dry she could barely swallow, and her mouth felt like the bottom of a chalk quarry. She was certain her tongue was swollen, and she was terrified she might choke to death. One thing was very clear: She was incapable of even a whisper, much less of enough noise to alert Sadie that she was there.

Judging from the bangs and creaks overhead, Sadie was

attacking the housework with unusual vigor. There was no point in wasting her energy now, since any sound would be impossible to hear above the noise Sadie was making. She would have to wait until she heard the maid come downstairs, and then find a way to attract her attention.

The door was on her left. If she could get close enough to it, perhaps she could rock the chair against it. She could feel no sensation in her hands and feet. She could only pray that she had the strength to move the chair.

Concentrating all her thoughts to that end, she pushed down on her feet and shoved hard.

It was as if she had pushed through a cloud. She could feel the muscles in her thighs straining, but her legs might have been cut off at the knees for all the use they were. Again and again she stamped on the floor, hoping to get the blood circulating enough to give her momentum.

Aware of the time slipping away, she gritted her teeth and stamped harder. After what seemed like hours, she began to feel an unpleasant tingle in her calves. Heartened by the small sign, she rocked back and forth, back and forth, stamping as hard as she could.

A door slammed overhead. Then followed the sound she had dreaded. The stairs creaked again as Sadie stomped down them. Frantic now, Elizabeth rocked harder. She managed to tip the back legs high enough to hit lightly on the floor.

The creaking stopped midway, as if Sadie had paused.

Hope driving her on, Elizabeth rocked and rocked. Faster and faster she bounced, while she summoned every last bit of air in her lungs to cry out.

Her throat stung with the effort, and her back felt as if it were breaking in two. In a final desperate effort, with all of her strength, she threw her entire body forward and then back. The chair poised precariously on two legs for a breathless moment, then crashed backward onto the floor.

Elizabeth's head met the wall with a resounding crack. The last thing she heard was Sadie's scream as she rushed down the rest of the stairs.

"Here you go, then, eat your soup." Violet placed two steaming bowls on the kitchen table in front of the two youngest girls, then returned to the stove for the third. The feeling of dread that had been with her ever since last night made her entire body feel heavy, slowing her down. In an effort to shake off her fear, she concentrated on the girls again. "If you're good, I'll let you take the dogs out onto the lawn this afternoon."

"Can we play tennis?" Patsy eyed the bowl of soup being set in front of her. "We saw the tennis court this morning, and Martin said he'd ask the master if we could play."

Jenny started dropping pieces of bread into her soup. "Who's the master? Is he going to eat with us?"

"Not unless he climbs out of his grave to do it," Violet said dryly. "The master's dead. Killed in a bombing raid three years ago in London."

Patsy gave her a solemn look. "Our mum's in London."

Violet caught her breath. "Oh, lovey, I'm so sorry. I forgot. Well, don't you worry. The bombs won't get your mother, I'm sure of it. In any case, she's coming down here to get you this very afternoon. I was keeping it as a surprise, but you might as well know now. She'll be here in a couple of hours."

All three girls stared at her with wide eyes.

"How'd she know we was here?" Patsy demanded.

"I rang the War Office in London. They rang me back a little while ago and said they'd arranged for your mother to come down here and get you."

"We're going back to London?" Maureen's face was red with excitement, and Jenny went on eating her soup with a satisfied smile on her face.

Patsy looked worried. "What about the bombs?"

"Well, things are not as bad as they were when you

left. Your mother probably has an air raid shelter in the garden by now, so you'll all be safe. Now eat your—"

She froze as the door suddenly crashed open so hard it banged against the wall. Sadie stood in the doorway, her face as white as the pillowcases on the line outside.

"What in the world is the matter with you?" Violet demanded. "You look as if you've seen a ghost."

Sadie just stood there, opening and shutting her mouth without any sound coming out of it.

Worried now, Violet dropped the soup ladle and hurried toward her. "Here, sit down a minute. What's happened?" A dreadful thought struck her, and her entire body went cold. "Is it her ladyship? Is it Lady Elizabeth? Sadie? Sad-a-a-y!" She took hold of her arm and shook it hard. "Tell me what's happened!"

Jenny started to cry, and Patsy put a scrawny arm around her. The sound seemed to shake Sadie out of her daze. She started wailing like a cat in heat. "Ooh, it was awful . . . really, really awful. I was so scared. I'm never going back there. Never."

"What? What were you scared of?"

A deep voice spoke from behind Violet. "Is everything all right here?"

Violet straightened, and met the concerned gaze of Major Monroe. "Oh, Major, I'm glad you're here. Sadie's had some kind of scare, and I'm afraid it has something to do with Lady Elizabeth."

"It ain't got nothing to do with her ladyship," Sadie said breathlessly. "It's that blasted cottage. It's blinking *haunted!* There's ghosts in there!" Her voice rose on the last word, and all three children stared at each other in fright.

Violet frowned at the maid in disgust. "Haunted? *Haunted?* You scared the daylights out of me because you thought you saw a blinking ghost? What's the matter with you? Been talking to that crazy old goat, Martin, I don't doubt. Now listen here, my girl—"

Sadie bolted out of her chair. "Don't you 'my girl' me,

you bloody idiot. I know a ghost when I hear one. I was
walking down the stairs in that old cottage, and I heard it
bumping around. Heard it as plain as day. But I couldn't
see it. I heard it right on the stairs with me. Right *next* to
me, it was, and there weren't nothing there. It was invis-
ible, that's what. Bloody good job, too, if you ask me. I
hate to think what it looked like if I'd seen it. Great big
hairy monster with glowing red eyes. . . ."

Jenny and Maureen screamed in unison, and Violet
started so violently she banged her elbow on the stove.
"Shut up, Sadie, for Gawd's sake. You're scaring the
girls."

"What cottage was this?"

Earl's words, spoken in a voice of reason, seemed to
calm everyone down, though Sadie still sounded shaky
when she answered.

"It's the end cottage on Sandhill Lane. It's empty, and
her ladyship wanted me to clean it. Well, I went down
there, didn't I—"

"Fred Bickham's cottage," Violet said, interrupting her.
"Wait a minute. Is it possible . . . ?"

"Anything's possible." Earl glanced at the clock. "Tell
me how to get there, and I'll take a look."

"I'm going with you," Violet said firmly. "Sadie, keep
an eye on the girls. Their mother should be arriving here
in an hour or two. With any luck, I'll be back by then."

Earl was already half out the door, and she hurried after
him. If it was Lizzie that Sadie had heard, then at least
she was still alive. There was hope, after all.

It was Violet's first ride in a jeep, and in any other circumstances, she would have found the experience quite
thrilling. Right now, however, all she could think about
was what they might find at the cottage. She kept going
over and over what Sadie had said. *I heard it right on the
stairs with me. Right next to me, it was, and there weren't
nothing there.*

"The room under the stairs," she said, shouting into the

wind that whipped the words from her mouth as Earl sped down the hill at breakneck speed.

"What?" He glanced at her, then back at the road.

"Under the stairs. It's where we're supposed to hide in a raid. That's why Sadie heard it on the stairs. Somehow Lizzie must have got locked inside." Her heart sank when she remembered something. "No, wait, she can't be. It locks from the inside."

Earl didn't answer, but his expression darkened. Minutes later his jeep swung into the lane on two wheels and came to a screeching halt in front of the cottage.

For a bad moment Violet thought they'd have to break in, since she'd forgotten to get the key from Sadie. She needn't have worried, however. The front door stood wide open. Sadie must have been so scared she'd flown right out of there.

Violet let Earl go in ahead of her, and he headed straight for the hallway. Sadie's bucket lay on its side at the foot of the stairs, with dusters and tins of cleaning powder scattered all around it.

Violet watched Earl hook his fingers around the handle and tug open the door. All she could see was a triangle of light from the hallway spilling into the dark space, and what looked like a bundle of clothes lying just beyond.

Then Earl muttered something she didn't catch. Bowed low, he ducked into the narrow space and began tugging on whatever was lying there. After a moment of grunting, he called out, "Can you get in here to give me a hand?"

Violet leaned over his back and peered inside. As her eyes adjusted to the gloom, she saw what he had seen. "Oh, God," she breathed. "Please, let her be alive."

Elizabeth slowly opened her eyes, and far more quickly closed them again. The light hurt, though she couldn't think why. She'd opened her eyes to the sunlight in this room for as long as she could remember. Why was this morning different?

"She's awake," Violet's voice said by her side. "Polly, go and tell the major."

Now she knew why the sun hurt her eyes. Usually, when she woke up, the blackout curtains hid the glare. And the sun was awfully low for morning. Warily, she opened her eyes again.

"How are you feeling, ducks?" Violet asked, sounding different, somehow. "Better, are you?"

Elizabeth tried to answer, but her throat was on fire and her tongue seemed to be stuck to the roof of her mouth.

"Here," Violet said. Her arm slid under Elizabeth's shoulders and she raised her head. "Drink this. We've had the devil of a time getting water down you. It'll be easier now you're awake. Oops, spilled a drop, didn't you? Never mind. Just keep on drinking. A little at a time, the doctor says."

"Doctor?" Elizabeth formed the word, though it came out in a dreadful rasp. She must have had the flu or something.

"You had a nasty bump on the head, and you were dehydrated, but Dr. Sheridan says with a bit of rest you'll be as good as new." Violet gave her a sharp look. "You had a narrow escape, my girl. If it hadn't been for the major, you could be dead by now. I tell you, when he carried you out of there, lying so limp in his arms, I thought you *were* dead. I hope you've learned your lesson, that I do."

Elizabeth blinked. Now she remembered. Bit by bit it was coming back to her. "Reggie Stewart," she said painfully.

"The constables got him this afternoon in Southampton. Trying to get on a boat to Ireland, he was. They locked him up down there, though George said he'll probably come back to North Horsham for his trial. You know where they found the hammer he used to smash that poor man's face in? Buried in the Victory Garden. In all the excitement, nobody thought to dig the rest of it up." She shook her head. "You must have walked in on him. Must have been a dreadful shock for you to see him still alive."

Elizabeth sipped some more water from the cup Violet held. "No, I knew he was alive," she said hoarsely. "When I was at the funeral this morning and—"

"The funeral was yesterday, Lizzie. You've been asleep since then. It's Tuesday evening."

Elizabeth frowned, trying to remember exactly what happened. "Well, I saw Reggie at the funeral, and I followed him back to the cottage."

"Go on!" Violet put the cup down. "What was he doing at the funeral? I wonder who they were burying, then?"

"That was Fred Bickham." Elizabeth closed her eyes. "I'm sorry, but my head really hurts, and I can't think straight. I'll tell you the whole story later."

"Of course, dearie. You rest now. You've been—" She broke off as a light tap came on the door. "Just a minute."

Elizabeth watched her cross the room to the door and open it. "Oh, there you are, Major. Yes, she's fine. Sounds like a frog with pneumonia, but I'm sure she'll be right as rain in a day or two."

Elizabeth heard Earl's deep voice say something.

Violet glanced back at her. "Oh, I don't think that's a good idea, Major. I mean, she's really tired, and it wouldn't be proper for you to be in her bedroom."

Elizabeth pulled in a breath, and as firmly as she could manage, said, "Violet, let him in."

Violet tutted, but opened the door wider. "Just for a moment then, Major. She needs her rest."

Elizabeth smiled at the tall figure entering the room. There really was something about an American uniform that did wonderful things for a man. "I understand that once again I have you to thank for my rescue," she said, drawing the sheets up to her chin.

He grinned, and sat down in the chair next to her. "It's becoming quite a habit. You've got to stop scaring me like this."

"Sorry. I suppose it was a silly thing to do. I'd started to suspect that Reggie might still be alive, and I was going to stop the funeral, but I wasn't certain until Joshua told me it was the first time he'd seen Reggie's nails clean, and then I was certain it wasn't Reggie, and with Fred being missing, I guessed it was him they were burying, and then I saw someone who appeared to be Fred at the funeral and I knew it couldn't be, so it had to be Reggie, and I followed him and that's when—"

Her voice, which had been getting raspier with each sentence, finally gave out altogether.

"Whoa, there, tiger," Earl said softly. "You never did know when to stop yakking. Here, take a drink. You've got a lot to catch up on."

"I do?"

"Well, let's see . . . Sam Cutter is out of the hospital and recuperating in the east wing. . . ."

"I imagine Polly is happy about that."

Earl shrugged. "I think he's giving her a tough time, but she seems determined to hang in there."

"Jolly good for her."

"Then there's the three little guests who've been haunting the manor."

Elizabeth looked at him in alarm. "Ghosts? You saw them?"

Earl laughed. "Not ghosts. *Guests.* But I'll fill you in on all that later. Right now you need a drink, then a long rest. When you feel better, we'll talk."

She started to protest, but then forgot all about her questions, for this time it was *his* arm sliding under her shoulders to raise her head, and she wanted nothing in her mind to distract her from the pure pleasure of the moment.